The Tycoon's Secretive Temptress

Elizabeth Lennox

Chapter 1

The soft ping of the elevator's arrival was her only warning.

Even the faint sounds of his confident footsteps were muted by the thick carpeting on the executive hallway but...she knew. Gianna knew *exactly* who had just stepped off that elevator. Not because she could feel him, hear him, or because the scent of his spicy aftershave preceded his presence.

Nope. She knew who was coming down the long, silent hallway because it was seven fourteen in the morning. Every morning at exactly ten minutes past seven, Brant Jones drove his sleek Mercedes into the mostly-empty parking lot. At eleven minutes past seven, he stepped through the doors of the corporate headquarters for Rembrandt Cosmetics, walking across the impressive lobby, but already looking pre-occupied, ready to tackle the world. The elevator ride up to the executive floor absorbed the next three minutes.

After working for the man for the past several months, Gianna knew that she could set her watch to his arrival. Every morning, there was absolutely no deviation from the man's rigid routine.

Twisting the rubber band around with her fingers, she idly wondered what he would do if she snapped the band across the hallway and...!

NO! No, no, no, no, no! With horror, she watched as the rubber band soared over the thick carpet, landing beside a very expensive pair of loafers.

Darn it!

"Bored again, Gianna?"

That deep, gravelly voice vibrated through her. A part of her wanted to figure out how to make the man smile. Another part wanted to piss him off. Unfortunately, those opposing impulses seemed to wage a constant battle in her head. And equally unfortunate was her lack of filter, which meant that she tended to act on those unfortunate, unwise impulses.

"Um..."

Quickly, Gianna shoved the papers under a stack of files. When she looked up at him, his frown deepened. Gianna could see the suspicion in his handsome features and moved quickly to distract him.

"Did you have a good morning?" she asked, her smile bright and hopeful.

He glanced from the stack of files to her face, his gaze narrowing with...something strange. Distrust?

"In my office, Gianna," Brant Jones snapped. Those shoes turned and walked down the hallway towards the posh executive offices.

Gianna stood up slowly, giving him time to move ahead her. No point in creating additional naughty, ill-advised temptation in her head, she lectured herself. As for watching the man's broad shoulders...well, the ideas that occurred to her simply weren't professional or appropriate.

Moments later, she stepped into his office and stood there, waiting for...something.

"Close the door," Brant ordered. Gianna considered defying the command, not sure if she wanted to be alone with the man in his current mood. It might be better if there were witnesses to her murder.

Then she caught his glare and all of those deliciously naughty ideas came flooding back to her. That need to get a rise out of Brant Jones, to make him feel...something, anything other than disdain for her, hit her hard. So as she reached for the door, their eyes locked. He anticipated her act and glared harder, daring her to follow through. Wrong thing to do, Gianna thought gleefully. A challenge? Oh, she was always up for a challenge! Especially where this man was concerned.

Slam!

There! Door closed, she thought with satisfaction. And noise! Goodness, the loud noise inside this stuffy office felt liberating!

As she watched, his irritation grew.

Brant didn't say anything for a long moment. He simply stared at her. Like a bug. A huge, creepy bug crawling across his immaculate, expensive carpet. His immaculate, noise-silencing carpet! How about a tile floor, she thought as she waited for his furious inspection to end.

"Why would I install tile?"

Gianna blinked, cringing inwardly. She hadn't meant to say that out loud. Darn filter! What's the point of having a filter if it didn't work?!

"Um...just...sound." Giving in to her desperation, she moved forward slightly, her hands lifting into the air imploringly, speaking as much with her hands as with her words, as any good Italian woman tended to do. "Don't you ever want some noise? Something to let you know that you're alive and that the world is moving around?" She spun around, unaware of her skirt lifting with the movement, giving her boss a glimpse at her legs. Sighing as she took in the amazing view of the mountains from his massive office, she spun back to face him once again. "In this silent room, it is oppressive! You have a gorgeous view of the Rocky Mountains and yet," her arm swept the air, indicating his massive desk and leather chair, "you work with your back to the resplendent view!"

Brant settled slowly in said leather chair, making sure that he didn't look down at her legs…again. It was always a delight to watch Gianna talk, her wild, dark curls dancing around her delicate features. Even listening to her was amazing. Her English was brilliant. Her words were tinged with a beautiful, lilting, Italian accent. He almost laughed at her use of 'resplendent' but swallowed the urge, not wanting to offend her. He knew that she constantly pushed to improve her use of the language by trying out new words and phrases. Sometimes her new words were right on target and other times, they weren't. Either way, she was like a breath of crisp, fresh air. A freshness that he loved, even though she made him crazy. There was something about her…she hid things from him, such as the papers she'd shoved under the files moments ago. And yet, her work was always perfect. Was he only imagining that? Was he looking for ways to not trust her? He wasn't used to women affecting him the way Gianna did, and yet he couldn't seem to stop noticing…well, noticing every damn thing about her!

Unfortunately, she was bored. He knew that she needed better challenges, more intellectual stimulation, but no matter how many assignments he handed over to her, she finished them with ease and accuracy, wanting more. She was doing the jobs of three people at the moment. Yet she still didn't have enough to keep her busy.

Still, her attitude and pranks were…well, he couldn't take it easy on her. There was a professionalism within the company that needed to be maintained. "Your father asked me to hire you, Gianna. He wanted you to work, not redecorate my office."

She stomped across the office, obviously offended by the

comment. "I work! But that's all anyone does here! They work! No one does anything *interesting*!" She huffed for a moment, then swung around. "Where is the fun? Where is the laughter? You Americans!" she sighed with an inelegant snort. "You never do anything *fun*! You all work too hard and never stop to enjoy all of life's glorious gifts! Even in your off time, you run and exercise, not taking time to relax and simply enjoy the sunrise or sunset!"

Brant leaned back in his chair, images of the fun things he'd like to do with her dancing in his mind. He'd start with taking off that sexy wrap dress that clung to her voluptuous figure. With one light tug of that silk bow at her tiny waist, the dress would fall open. One tug and he would be able to see all her lush curves. At twenty-five, Gianna had an Italian sense of style which was so different from the comparatively conservative American looks. The flamboyant colors and simple lines contributed to the sensuousness of whatever she wore. Add her dramatic flair for everything and it was no wonder Brant was hooked. Completely!

Not that he would do anything about it. She was gorgeous and outrageous, flagrantly taunting him some days and others, annoying him by simply walking down the office hallways. Knowing that he couldn't touch her made him grit his teeth. And the hiding! He couldn't forget about whatever it was that she hid under the files the moment he looked into her office.

Blinking, he focused back on the present. She'd asked him a question. Question? No, she'd made a comment. Something about...Americans? Yeah, that was it. She thought that Americans were boring and work driven. Oh, if only she could see his thoughts, she'd know full well that he was focused on her at the moment. Work? Hell, at the moment, he had no idea what was on his desk or on his calendar. His entire thought process was focused on Gianna and that damn bow at her waist!

On the other hand, Brant was fully aware of the enticing

shadow between her breasts and her slender ankles. Pulling his eyes back up to her darker ones, he nodded in agreement, trying to remember the topic of conversation. "Yes. Americans work hard."

"Why?!" she gasped, throwing her hands up in the air again. That dramatic Italian flair never ceased to amaze him. "Why can't you just take a day off and…" she gestured toward the mountains, "go have a picnic! Luxuriate in the beauty around you! Take a bubble bath or drink some wine!"

"You want me to take a bubble bath?" he teased. Gianna didn't understand that he was teasing her and her disgust escalated. Which only amused him further.

She wagged a finger at him. "You're such an American! You take everything so actually!"

"Literally," he corrected in what he hoped was a gentle tone.

"Exactly!"

He didn't explain. Why bother? He liked it when she messed up a word or phrase. He thought it was adorable, just like the rest of her. And besides, her grasp of the English language was leaps and bounds better than his grasp of Italian. Although, he'd started looking up a few words, trying to figure out what she occasionally muttered under her breath.

Focusing back on their conversation, he said, "So, you want to go on a picnic?"

She swung around and he again had to stifle a chuckle as she glared at him. Obviously, his intimidating nature didn't affect her like it affected the rest of his staff. The woman was courageous, he'd give her that much.

"A picnic would be lovely, but it isn't the only thing that would brighten a day!"

He tapped his fingers on his desk. Damn, he loved it when her accent deepened. He could gauge her emotions by the intensity of her accent. Right at this moment, she was angry, but even that turned him on.

Ignoring his body's increasing reaction to her lush figure and sparkling eyes, he cocked an eyebrow. "Other suggestions?"

She frowned thoughtfully, her hands coming to rest on her rounded hips. "You are mocking me." With a sigh, she looked up at the ceiling, then back at him. Thankfully, he was able to bring his eyes back up to hers before she noticed he was surveying her breasts. The dress was made of some sort of stretchy material. It was literally straining at the seams as the material struggled to keep her lush curves encased.

"I'm not mocking you. Your father asked me to take care of you."

She stomped a foot and he wondered what she would do if he lifted her into his arms and....

"My father asked you to *employ* me for this next year."

"And take care of you." He only said it to irritate her further. And yeah, he liked it when she wiggled like that. Brant struggled, and failed, to keep his eyes on her face. What else could a man to do when she moved like that? Did she have any idea of how erotic it was when she did that? Everything moved! Every sensuous, gorgeous, sexy part of her figure drew his attention! And yeah, his eyes drifted lower, taking it all in. He was only human after all.

"No! No man takes care of me! One *takes care* of babies and children! I take care of myself! I refuse to allow any man to take care of me!"

Brant ignored this assertion because he had communicated with Gianna's father every week since she'd arrived two months ago. The man worried about his daughter and demanded regular updates on her welfare from Brant.

"Did you finish the report I sent to you yesterday?" he asked, changing the subject.

She shrugged dismissively. "Yes. Your sales are down in the West Coast by two percent, but up dramatically in the East Coast," she explained. "Eleven point one percent, actually." She swung around to look at him. "The trainer on the east is wonderful. Selena trained that team good and they know how to suggest individual products more better."

Brant leaned back in his chair, enjoying the errors in her language as well as the accent. He listened as Gianna recited specifically which products were more closely aligned with another and which upsold best. It was an easy, service-oriented way of selling more by simply suggesting the client purchase mascara remover when they bought mascara. Or suggesting makeup primer when they wanted foundation. It was simple to explain how primer allowed a customer to use less makeup and help it last all day, thereby saving them money in the long term. And Gianna's lilting accent only made the recitation even more interesting.

As she recited the details from memory, all of his suspicions were pushed away. She was an outstanding employee, he thought. If he had some salacious thoughts, then he'd just have to be more disciplined about his interactions with her.

Gianna, with her brilliant mind and impressive ability to recall, knew the figures for each section of the country and the profit margins for each product off the top of her head. So not only had she done the research, she knew exactly how to improve top-line revenue in the areas that had lower sales. Her analysis wasn't just numbers. It was extraordinary!

She had more than earned a promotion. Even if she was only here for the year, the woman's intelligence and insight deserved more responsibility and more money – and less of his unfounded suspicions. "So, what do you suggest?"

"Get the East Coast trainer out to the West Coast and train

the trainers more effectively," she replied, as if the solution was obvious.

He'd already made a note to do so. For the next hour, he asked detailed questions and she answered them without hesitation, including statistics and data to back up each of her suggestions. She'd been hired to work in the financial department under Brant's chief financial officer, but the information she had provided was far better than what his CFO, Ken, had provided yesterday. Ken only presented the raw numbers, not the analysis behind the numbers. Ken was good, but Gianna was better. Ken's analysis wasn't as thorough, nor could he spout the data off the top of his head as Gianna could and did.

His assistant Todd rapped timidly on the door, interrupting their enlightening and fascinating conversation.

"What is it?" Brant snapped, ignoring the way Todd cringed slightly at the fierceness in his tone.

"I apologize for interrupting, sir, but your first meeting of the morning has convened."

Brant eyes slashed to the computer monitor, surprised that so much time had passed. Sure enough, there was a flashing message indicating that he was late for his first meeting. Unfortunately, his distraction was normal when Gianna was around.

He returned to Gianna, sitting in front of his desk. Her brown eyes glowed with defiance as her dark curls danced around her shoulders, her body vibrating with energy. What was it about Gianna...?

Her gaze challenged him to say she'd gotten anything wrong during their hour-plus conversation. And damn it, he really wanted to! He wanted to tell her to get the hell out of his office and his company. He wanted to order her back to Italy where her sense of vibrancy and beauty belonged. And yet, he also wanted her to stay right there in that chair so that he could talk to her, watch her animated features and just...be with her.

Gianna was a complication in his life that he didn't need or want. He absolutely refused admit that she was driving him to distraction. So, what if he looked forward to seeing her every damn morning? And there was no way he'd admit to anyone else that he enjoyed looking at her, talking with her. Listening to her.

Seeing her smile.

It made absolutely no sense. He had to remind himself that didn't trust her, he didn't like her, and he definitely didn't think she was beautiful. Even though she was. Stunningly beautiful! And damn, he hated the way her full lips softened like that, as if she might be thinking about kissing him like he thought about kissing her.

Kissing?

Wait. Huh?! What the hell? He never thought about kissing the damn woman! He wanted her gone! Out of his life!

And yet, his eyes lingered on those soft lips, wondering if she would vibrate with the same kind of energy if he made love to her. What would her lips do when she clim....!

"Sir?"

Brant glowered at his assistant, irritated that his concentration on Gianna's lips had been interrupted. "What?"

Yeah, he'd been reduced to this, he thought. Brant considered admonishing himself for looking, but Gianna's full, incredibly full, round breasts were...beautiful. And lush. There really was no other way to describe her. Tiny waist, full hips, and breasts that would be more than a handful.

She was too short, he told himself. At several inches over six feet, Brant preferred women to be tall and sultry, with more subtle curves. He liked athletic women, he reminded himself firmly. He wondered if Gianna played any sports. She had the kind of body men drool over, watch and stare at longingly.

Exactly as he was doing now.

Damn, she was also brilliant and funny. He needed to treat her with respect.

At least until he understood her motives for being here. Why would a woman like Gianna travel halfway around the world to work in Colorado at a cosmetics company? It just didn't make sense.

"Sir?"

Ignoring his timid assistant, he made a decision. With a flash of inspiration, Brant stood up. "Come with me," Brant ordered, taking the materials that Todd held out for him. "Make another copy of this for Ms. Lianar and bring it to the conference room. She'll sit in on the meeting."

He was at the door before he realized that Gianna was still sitting. "Are you coming?" he snapped.

Gianna leapt to her feet, grabbing catching her pen before it hit the floor and tucking it into her notebook. She straightened gracefully and nodded. *"Pronto!"* she replied, frowning slightly as she realized she'd slipped back to her native tongue. "Ready," she repeated in English. Although she had no idea what she was ready for, so in reality, she couldn't be ready. Especially not after that heated look! Her lips felt warmer than they should, almost as if she could already feel his kiss...

Wait! What was she thinking? Kissing Brant Jones? No! No way! Brant Jones was boring and tedious! He was completely un-kissable! He worked too hard and didn't know how enjoy life! He probably only had sex in missionary position...

Her gaze lingered on his shoulders before sliding down to his lean waist and long legs...

"Gianna!" he snapped.

Under other circumstances, she might have laughed and teased the man in question, trying to get him to lighten up and smile. But Brant Jones wasn't capable of smiling. She'd learned that over the past several weeks of working for him. He didn't smile, he never lightened up and his whole world revolved around Rembrandt Cosmetics, the company he and his brother owned.

When she'd applied for this position at the Denver based company, she had no idea that such an innovative, exciting company would be run by such a harsh, tediously boring man. He had no life outside of the building. She arrived in the office before he did most mornings, but he was here late into the night, working seventy or more hours a week. And that was just the hours she knew about. Gianna suspected that the man probably worked from home as well.

Hurrying after him, she let herself enjoy watching him walk down the hallway. He was deliciously tall with tantalizingly wide shoulders that a woman could lay her head upon and sigh with happiness. She could see the muscles rippling under the tailored dress shirt, tapering to a lean waist. There wasn't a spot of extra fat on his body.

What would his butt feel like? As she walked behind him, she examined his butt which was currently covered with well fitting, expensive material. She imagined her hand exploring...moving along the curve. Firm, she decided. Firm and incredible!

Just the thought of touching him caused her breath to catch. Gianna could definitely imagine her fingers moving over his back, his shoulders, his...

He paused to speak to someone, glancing at her as he turned and she froze. Did her face reveal what she'd been thinking? Goodness, she certainly hoped not!

Gianna waited while he spoke, continuing to enjoy her view.

Such a pity! The first time she'd seen him, Gianna had thought he was a god! He was so tall and masculine, so appealingly sexy. Then she'd gotten to know him. Now...okay, so he was still handsome and sexy, but she fought her attraction constantly. No way did she want a man like Brant Jones. He was boring. He didn't live life, he toiled it away, working long hours and never appreciating the beauty of the world. He might exercise like a demon to maintain that physique, but the man didn't know how to truly enjoy life. On top of all that, he was angry all the time.

Gianna wanted a man who smiled and laughed. A man who would take a day off, just because it was a beautiful day! Someone daring and adventurous.

"Here!" he pointed as he sat down at the head of the conference room table.

Gianna shivered at the hard authoritative tone even as she rebelled against it.

"Here?" she asked innocently, pointing at the chair.

"Yes. Sit." And he turned away as everyone hurriedly took their seats.

"I heel pretty well too, if you ask nicely," she whispered, settling into the chair he'd indicated.

Her words caught his attention and he turned his head, scowling at her. Unfortunately, he only paused long enough to make her knees feel all wobbly before turning back to the others in the room.

For several minutes, Gianna pretended to take notes, but she was actually admonishing herself for taunting him. Why couldn't she just leave well enough alone? Why did she have to...what was the American phrase? Poke the panda? That didn't sound right, but she shrugged, then looked up to find that the man in question was staring at her.

"Forgive, I was writing down what you said a moment ago. Was there a question?" she asked.

Once again, his eyes narrowed suspiciously. The man was very distrustful! Sheesh! Just because he was right, well, that didn't mean she was going to admit that to him!

Thankfully, Todd stepped into the room, handing her copies of the report everyone else already had in front of them. "Here you go," he whispered with a smile and a blush.

Gianna beamed gratefully up at him. "*Grazie!*" she whispered back.

Todd's smile widened in return and he actually tripped on his way out, but Gianna had already turned her attention back to Brant. She lifted her eyebrows curiously, wondering what she'd missed.

He sighed, rubbing his forehead and Gianna stared at his hands. They were strong hands. Long fingers. One of those fingers ran down a chart on the report the group was discussing and Gianna wondered what it would feel like to have that finger slide down her skin. She shivered at the images flashing through her mind.

Again, Brant stopped the meeting to glare at her.

Gianna's eyes widened with surprise and she lifted her hands in the air. "I said nothing," she responded defensively.

Another heavy sigh from him, or was that a growl? Several people brought up new information and Gianna forced her attention on the conversation. The meeting participants were discussing a new line of cosmetics and the best way to market them. Brant was the financial genius of the company, and Gianna thought it was hot when he started discussing numbers. Every time his deep voice started talking about variances or gross contribution, a shiver went through her. Odd, yes, but she didn't care. The man was sexy! Intelligence was hot and Brant Jones was smarter than average!

Or maybe it was just his deep voice. She'd read about the deep voices of American men but, until she'd met Brant Jones, no American man had come even close to that sexy, husky tone.

Italian men were good looking, but there was just something...
more...about Brant Jones. He was appealing in so many ways.

Unfortunately, he was also a fuddy duddy. Such a pity!

"Ms. Lianar will take over developing the budget for the launch,"
he announced abruptly.

Gianna sat up in her chair, startled. "I am?"

He turned and those dark eyes sizzled with challenge. "Think
you can handle it?"

Oh, he was good! Creating a budget for a new line would be...
exciting! So many issues, problems, and expenses! There would
be marking costs, advertising, capital expenses, indirect costs....oh,
glorious challenges! "Absolutely," she declared, eager to begin.

For the past several weeks, she'd been assigned tedious reports
that were nothing more than data entry. Gianna had earned a
master's degree in business administration from the prestigious
London School of Business. She'd come to the United States
wanting to dig deep into the numbers, truly challenge herself with
her knowledge. But so far, she'd been pushed into pathetically
basic roles that didn't test her abilities in any way.

This was different. Creating a budget for the entire launch
would be...oh, this was exciting!

"Excellent," the fuddy-duddy replied. Turning back to
the meeting participants, he continued, "Everyone, send your
requirements to Ms. Lianar. She'll have a budget ready for next
week's meetings complete with indirect impacts. Barbara, make
sure that you send Ms. Lianar the expenses you anticipate. Jeanie,
don't forget to include the distribution costs. We had problems
with that during the Magic perfume release last year."

"Yes, sir," Jeanie agreed, diligently writing notes.

Gianna frantically scribbled notes of her own. "Who will send
me the packaging, training, and promotional expenses?"

Was that a spark of admiration in his eyes? Gianna held her

breath for a split second, shocked at the thought. She was so used to his suspicion and anger, but admiration was pretty nice!

He gave several more instructions and they set a time to follow up next week.

Everyone stood up except Gianna, who leaned over her notebook, already lost in the challenge of setting up a budget for this new effort. Creating a budget was a proper challenge! There were so many variables, so many ways that the product launch could fail.

"You got this?" a deep voice asked.

Gianna looked up, startled to find that she was alone in the conference room with Brant.

Straightening, she nodded eagerly, still scribbling. "Yes. I have so many ideas!" she breathed, eager to get back to her tiny office and start building the spreadsheet. "I will keep you informed every step on the way. I will ensure that this is detailed enough to give you the background into my numbers."

He chuckled and the unexpected sound drew her gaze upward. He'd laughed? Brant Jones never laughed! She *made* him laugh?

Her eyes widened as her body tingled with that unwelcome awareness that seemed to be the status quo lately.

"Slow down and send me the data as you get it." With that, he walked out of the conference room, leaving her stunned.

Had he really laughed? Yes, it was just a small sound of amusement, and it had been at her expense. She was overly enthusiastic, but who wouldn't be, with such an exciting challenge in front of her? Still, giving him a reason to laugh was…nice. Really nice!

Chapter 2

"What's wrong?" Reid asked, stepping into his brother's office. It was late, and the office was almost empty. Brant sat in near darkness, but he hadn't even noticed the deepening shadows, too focused on trying to work.

Brant blinked and scowled at his brother. "Why would you think something is wrong?"

Reid chucked and leaned a shoulder against the door jam. "Because you have that throbbing vein going on the side of your head. Always a bad sign."

Brant stared at his older brother as if he'd lost his mind. But after a moment, he conceded that he was stressed, then sighed and tossed his pen to the middle of his desk, leaning back in the leather chair to stretch sore, stiff muscles. "I just gave Gianna the launch budget project."

Reid dropped into the chair in front of Brant's desk. The chair Gianna had used earlier today. But Reid didn't look nearly as enticing as she had.

"Isn't that what she's been asking for?"

Brant cringed, nodding as he glanced out the windows, but he still didn't see the Denver skyline or the lights of the city. He was thinking about Gianna's excitement when he'd announced she'd be taking on the budget process. "Yeah, those monthly variance reports I asked her to do were beneath her. She has good skills."

Reid shifted. "She has the credentials to do so much more, but you've been holding back on giving her responsibility.   You've never treated an employee like that before. What's going on?"

Brant stood up and walked over to the window, rubbing the back of his neck. The sun had set a long ago, but the lights of Denver lit up the night until the mountains created a dark, impenetrable barrier. Damn, he loved this city. He loved the mountains and the throbbing pulse of the growing, urban area. He loved that he could drive a half hour away and be surrounded by mountains, forest, and silence. Or he could walk a few blocks down the street from his house and find twenty restaurants, each with unique flavors and offerings. There was nowhere else like Denver!!

Or Gianna, he thought with a sigh.

"Is it because she's a woman?"

Brant swung around with that question, glaring at his brother. "Why the hell would you ask *that*? Seventy-five percent of our staff is female.   In a cosmetics company, it's essential to have women on the staff. Hell, any company should include at least fifty percent female staff. You know that men and women provide unique perspectives. Bringing them together only makes sense."

Reid held up his hands, laughing softly. "Hey, I agree with you. Preaching to the choir here. I'm just wondering why you're holding this particular woman back. You've never been reticent about pushing an employee when they obviously have the skills, talent, and desire to take on more. What's so special about Gianna?"

Brant sighed again, trying to figure it out himself. "I don't trust her."

"Because she's beautiful?"

Brant stiffened and had to hold back on grabbing his brother by the front of his shirt and punching him out. "Why the hell are you looking at Gianna?"

Reid's eyes widened. A moment later, he whistled. "So it's like that, huh?"

Brant glared at his brother, his fists clenching and unclenching. "I have no idea what you're talking about. But stop looking at Gianna. She's an employee and we treat our employees with *respect*!"

Reid lifted his hands in surrender. "Hey brother, I'm with you. I just want to understand. And by the flare of temper that happens every time I ask about her, I'm wondering if there's something going on between you two."

"Absolutely not!" Brant asserted forcefully. Although, the image of her soft breasts as she bent over to catch the pen this morning came to mind.

"Earth to Brant!" Reid called, waving a hand in front of Brant's nose.

Brant focused, then scowled at his brother. "Why are you here? Why aren't you home with Selena?" Usually, Reid hurried out of the office at the end of the work day, eager to be home with his new wife.

"Because, at the moment, you're more amusing. Besides, she went to a spin class. I'm meeting her in a few minutes."

"Don't you cook dinner most nights?"

Reid grinned happily. Brant's envy of his marriage amused him.

"You're annoying, you know that?" Brant grumbled, but in a light-hearted way. As much as he was annoyed by Reid's love for his wife, Brant wanted that too. He wanted a woman he could come home to, someone that made him *want* to leave work to be with. Selena was a lovely, softhearted woman who had stolen Reid's heart from the moment he met her several months ago when Reid flew out to discover the trainer that was ramping up sales and offering brilliant new marketing ideas.

"Yeah," Reid replied cheerfully, unconcerned with his brother's irritation. "I know. And I don't care either."

Brant turned away from his brother, not wanting to see the

happiness on his face, even though Reid deserved every moment of it.

"So, why don't you trust her?" Reid asked, bringing the subject back to the original topic.

Brant rubbed the back of his neck. "I don't know."

"Has she done or said something that would make you doubt her loyalty to the company?"

Was his brother seriously bringing logic into this conversation? "Not at all," he admitted. Although…why did she stuff papers under files or into her desk whenever he entered her office?

"So, what is it?"

Brant banished the issue, trying to focus on his brother. He turned and leaned a hip against his desk meditatively. "Why is she here? Gianna has the credentials to work anywhere. Why Denver? Why not in London or New York? She could be making so much more money as a hedge fund manager or investment manager. Why a cosmetics company?"

"People say the same thing about you and I running a cosmetics company," Reid reminded him.

Brant smiled, thinking back to the genesis of their idea. "Yeah, well, that was pretty brilliant of us." Brant and Reid had dumped all of their savings into the company. With their youngest brother, Mack's, contribution as well, they'd created a small line of products and gotten them into the market. They were high quality, innovative, and environmentally friendly. The company had taken off so strongly, he and Reid had barely been able to keep up with the demand. Long days and nights of building up the company had brought them to the point where they were a major player in the global cosmetics market. Brands that had previously scoffed at Rembrandt Cosmetics were now playing catch up. Stores that had originally declined to carry their products were now demanding more stock. It had been difficult, but they'd created a successful company.

"What? Deciding on the makeup we liked women wearing and producing it?" Reid laughed. "Yeah. We had a real spark there."

"I know that no one understands. But I like beautiful women and love the confidence they show when they feel beautiful."

"I know the company line, brother, but you haven't answered my question. What has you so suspicious about Gianna?"

He sighed, shaking his head slightly. "I don't know. There's just something about her that irks me."

"You mean, she keeps distracting you?"

"She just..." he shook his head, irritation igniting his temper. Throwing his hands in the air, Gianna-style, he tried to explain to Reid. "How the hell can she speak English so perfectly, and yet, she messes up every single idiomatic phrase? What the hell is up with that?"

Reid smiled, surprised by Brant's outburst. "I think it's amusing. Some might even call it enchanting."

Brant might think that, if he allowed himself to. But he wasn't. So he didn't. "And her clothes! Damn, she..." he stopped, realizing where he was going.

His brother's eyebrows lifted higher with his comment. "You can't really be irritated by the clothing she wears. There's absolutely nothing wrong with her clothes. They are similar to the outfits that every other woman in the office wears, although she prefers brighter, more dramatic colors."

Brant thought about it and, well, perhaps his brother was right. But the way Gianna wore her clothes was...different. Sexier! The woman carried herself in a way that...well, it was hot!

"You don't think...?" Brant started to say, only to stop himself.

"I don't," Reid responded firmly before Brant could even finish the sentence. "Have you ever sat down and talked with her? She's intelligent, funny, and incredibly charming."

Brant's stance turned confrontational in a flash. "How the hell do you know that she's charming?" Brant demanded, unconscious of the way his hands curled into fists at the thought.

Reid laughed, shaking his head. Standing up, he patted his brother on the shoulder. "Seriously, brother, you have it bad. Gianna and Selena are really good friends. Gianna comes over for dinner pretty often and I find her completely charming. But not in the way that you're assuming, so just back off before you take a swing at me and I have to hurt you."

Brant relaxed, relieved by that explanation. "As if you could," he replied to his brother's retreating back.

"Give Gianna a break!" Reid called before disappearing into his own office. He reappeared in the hallway moments later and Brant knew that he was heading home to Selena, ready to enjoy his evening.

Sighing, Brant thought about packing up and going home as well. But there wasn't a beautiful woman waiting for him at home with a welcoming smile and dark, chocolate eyes. Just a big, empty house.

"Hell, I should get a dog," he muttered. Then shook his head. That wouldn't be fair to the dog. He worked long hours and traveled often. Leaving the dog home along for that long would be cruel.

A cat? No. Not fair to leave a cat alone for that long either, he told himself, thinking about Cat, the feline that had adopted Reid several years ago. That kitty needed more attention than a dog at times. And no way did he want the 'gifts' that Cat left on Reid and Selena's doorsteps almost daily. The dead vermin were disgusting. Sweet because of Cat's intentions, but gross.

A fish? He wasn't a big fan of fish. Some people thought they were interesting but the thought of cleaning their water regularly was just...

He needed a woman. Brant thought of the several ladies he could call. Any of them would happily meet him somewhere for dinner, they could enjoy a bottle of wine, and he could spend the rest of the evening enjoying her company.

And yet...the image of dark eyes flashing a challenge popped into his mind and he dismissed the idea of another woman. As he looked around his office, staring at the now-dark window, his disinterest in anyone other than Gianna irritated him because now she was distracting him from a night of pleasure.

How could she get under his skin so easily? What was it about her that made him...!

He didn't allow himself to finish the thought. Instead, he walked over to his desk and forced himself to focus on the numbers. Work would solve the issue, like it did every issue. And if Gianna was doing something unethical, if all of that paper hiding was an issue, he'd figure it out eventually. He'd just keep a close watch on her work and ensure that she didn't steal any proprietary information that she could pass along to another company when she moved back to Italy after her time here in Denver was over.

Chapter 3

"*Questo non funziona!*" Gianna groaned. "Why are you messing me up?' she demanded of the computer. "You no give me the answers I need!"

A few more keystrokes and she lowered her head to her hands, trying to regain her scattered focus.

It was Saturday morning and she was alone in the office. The silence was overwhelming, making her groans of frustration even more obvious.

Looking back up at the computer screen, she accepted that she didn't know how to get it to work properly. "One solution only," she muttered with increasing irritation.

Picking up the report, she carried it down the long, silent hallway. It might be Saturday, a time to be out in the world enjoying the sunshine and fresh air, but she knew that Brant would be here. He was always here, she thought with increasing trepidation.

But as soon as she reached his office, the silence was complete. No Brant. "He is not here?" She stepped into his office. "*Perche?*"

With a huff, she pulled out her cell phone and texted him. "Having problems. Why you not here at the office to help?"

She stuffed her cell phone back in her pocket and headed to her office, determined to figure this problem out. If the great Brant Jones wasn't here, then he was most likely doing something tediously boring and wouldn't answer her text. The man could focus on something and lose track of the world, she knew.

So she was startled when her phone vibrated. She read the

reply. "Bring the reports to me. I'll look them over." And he sent her an address.

Gianna's heart rate sped up. Was this his home? Where he slept? Did he sleep in the nude? She pictured him sprawled across a bed, a sheet casually draped over his body and one muscular arm flung across his eyes.

Her heart tripped over its feet at the thought of going to his house where he might, she hoped, sleep naked.

And then reality came rushing back, crushing her dreams and banishing images of Brant naked. It probably wasn't his house. And if it was, then he was working in his home office.

Gianna snorted. "And you are here," she pointed out to the silent room. "Why you not out enjoying the sunshine?" she asked of herself. "You tease him about having no life," she grumbled, picking up her papers and laptop, stuffing everything into her leather tote. "And yet, you have no life now! You are becoming too American!"

Gianna giggled at the possibility. "Only in my dreams!" she sing-songed as she left the silent office. The elevator appeared immediately since no one was around to call it to another floor. The speed with which the elevator brought her to the parking garage was unprecedented. Unfortunately, she wasn't mentally prepared to see the man in question, even though she'd texted him for help. Telling herself she should have waited until Monday to ask for help, Giana flung her tote into the trunk of her hatchback. Asking for help in the office seemed normal. Brant providing that help in his home seemed much more...intimate!

Punching in the address to her GPS, she wondered what his home office was like. Boring, she decided immediately. "No color," she elaborated out loud, pressing the "Go" button that would initiate the directions from the car's computer. "No color and no art. The man is like mud."

As she pulled out of the parking garage, following the directions from the GPS, Gianna laughed at her imagination. The man wasn't mud. He was like a sculpture. A handsome, amazing sculpture that she wanted to run her hands over and discover why he was so cold and unfeeling. "The man is a *macchina*! A machine that runs on grouchiness!"

It took her less than ten minutes to find the address. And even more shocking, as she pulled into the driveway, the man in question was not inside working in a dreary home office. In fact, he was in soft, well-worn jeans that rode low on his hips and a grease stained tee shirt that hugged his muscular arms, shoulders, and chest.

Gianna sat in her car, the engine idling as she drank in the view. Never in her wildest imagination had she pictured Brant Jones in anything other than a pristine, tailored business suit. He often took the suit jacket off at work, even rolled up the sleeves of his white dress shirt, but that was the extent of his relaxation. He never even loosened his tie during the work day.

So seeing him, not only without the suit, but with grease on his shirt and...on his jeans as well, everything inside of her throbbed with awareness. Awareness and...something else. Something terrifying.

He watched her watching him, a dark eyebrow lifting in question as she continued to sit in her car. When she realized that she was making a fool of herself, she shook herself mentally. Shutting off the engine, she carefully stepped out of her car, unable to pull her eyes away.

"You..." her eyes dropped to his hands. Just two days ago, she'd admired them. Now they were covered in grease and... "You are holding a... *chiave inglese*," she snapped her fingers in frustration. "I know not the English word."

Brant looked down at his hand, lifting the tool up slightly. "A wrench?"

Her eyes widened, her mind absorbing the word. "Yes. You… You know not how to use that, *si?*" she asked with breathless hope.

He rolled his eyes. "Why would I be holding something I don't know how to use?" he asked, walking over to one of those big, red tool boxes that were so massive, they rolled around on wheels. He grabbed a rag and started wiping the grease from the wrench first, then his hands.

"What do you use that on, then?" she asked.

He pointed the wrench to something behind him. "That."

Gianna followed the line of his arm and the wrench and gasped when she saw the massive motorcycle behind him. It wasn't new. In fact, the beautiful machine looked rusty and old. "You are…" she looked up at him as she reverently walked over to the bike, "fixing this? No, no, that's not right. What's the word?"

"Restoring it. Yes." He moved over to it, running his hand along the chrome. "It's a 1950s Triumph Classic. She was just sitting in a woman's shed until about a year ago when I found it and bought it from her."

Gianna reached out to touch it, but jerked her hand back, looking up at him for permission. "May I?" she asked, awed by the beauty of the vintage motorcycle.

"Of course," he replied easily, moving to the other side of the bike.

She reached out, running her fingers along the smooth lines. She bent down low, admiring the engine, and caressing the brittle leather of the seat. "This is beautiful, Brant. You on a bike," she said, then shook her head. "I can't see you there."

"You can't picture me riding a motorcycle? Why? Do I not seem like a gear-head?"

She turned, frowning at him in confusion over the new word. "Explain?"

27

"A gear-head," he teased, bending down to rub his thumb over one of the engine lines. "A guy who likes to work on engines."

Gianna was entranced by his thumb, the way it caressed the chrome and the lines so gently. Would he touch a woman with that kind of reverence? She thought not. He...she turned and caught him watching her.

Like always, when he looked at her, her knees weakened, her heart pounded into overdrive.

"Do you..." she looked up at him, then down at the motorcycle. "You don't drive it, do you?" she sighed, longing to feel the power of the motorcycle. "You probably are going to display it in your living room, no?"

For a long moment, Brant didn't say anything. He didn't even move. He simply stared at her and she shifted uneasily, feeling as if she'd insulted him somehow. She wasn't trying to insult him. In fact, just the opposite.

"It isn't a bad thing," she blurted, feeling bad all of a sudden. "I mean...some people consider a bike like this a work of art." She caressed the seat lovingly. Still silence and she wasn't sure what to say. "I'm sorry, I didn't mean to insult you. Truly," she bowed her head slightly, trying to think of...

A helmet appeared in her line of sight. She stared at it for a long moment, trying to make sense of it. When she looked up at him, he stood there, holding the helmet patiently.

"Put it on, Gianna."

She licked her lips even as she accepted the helmet, her fingers digging into the soft cushioning of the interior. "Why?"

He didn't answer. He grabbed another helmet down from a shelf that she hadn't noticed. He put on the helmet and handed her a jacket, then flung a leather jacket over himself. "You'll need this too," he warned.

With a yelp of excitement, she held the helmet between her

knees as she put the jacket on, zipping it all the way up. It was too big for her and had probably been left at his house by another woman, but Gianna didn't care. Not one bit! She was going for a ride on a vintage motorcycle behind none other than Brant Jones! Who would have thought he had it in him?! Apparently, Selena had been right! Brant wasn't the tedious, boring accounting type with a barren soul. He had a bit of oomph to him after all!

He was already on the bike when she pushed the helmet down over her curls, tucking everything in before jumping on behind him.

"*Che emozione!*" she whispered, trying to temper her excitement but it was an uphill battle. The motorcycle, along with Brant's intoxicating presence, was overwhelming. As soon as he whipped the motorcycle pedal, revving the engine, she threw her head back, laughing with delight!

Brant couldn't believe what he was doing. Seeing Gianna outside the office was bad enough. As soon as she'd driven up in that sporty little roadster, he'd known that he was in trouble. Then she'd stepped out of the car in tight jeans and leather, high-heeled boots. Damn, she was a mighty fine looking woman! His blood was boiling with lust. Feeling her arms around his waist was... incredible! Even through the two layers of leather, he could still feel her breasts pressing against his back. And her legs on either side of his hips was making him want to turn around and pull her into him so he could make love to her, right there on the bike.

Damn it, why had she shown appropriate appreciation for his bike?! Seeing her admiring eyes move over the classic bike with that awed look in her eyes, he'd just...well, done the stupidest thing he'd ever done in his life.

It was the comment about putting his bike on display. That had thrown him over the edge, he decided as he slowed for traffic on interstate twenty-four. Traffic was heavy this afternoon and the sun warm. The leather jacket and bike helmet were miserable in this kind of stop and go traffic but…

He smiled, feeling her pull away from him. She was expecting him to weave in and out of traffic on the bike. Yeah, this traffic was annoying but…

The car in front of him moved ahead and he knew that there was only one more exit before he could leave the city. The rest of the traffic would clear and they could speed up. Another break, another few feet, and then several cars in front of him exited. Finally, the road ahead cleared out.

Brant heard as much as felt her sigh of boredom. Turning his head, he said, "Lean into me on the turns. It will help me balance." He felt her nod, but she didn't really hold onto him. Ready to teach her a lesson, he gunned the engine. Immediately, her arms grabbed hold of him again. He felt her press her breasts against his back. Grinning, he increased the speed and they both leaned into the wind.

Yeah, this was what riding a motorcycle was all about. It was the open road, the mountains in the distance and a woman's body against his. He felt Gianna's breasts against his back and her inner thighs pressing against his legs. Damn, she felt good!

Speeding up even more, he could literally feel her excitement even though he couldn't hear anything beyond the wind and engine.

Twenty minutes later, he turned off and headed towards the mountains. Winding mountain roads were a lot of fun. He'd never take these roads if it were raining or snowing. The bike wouldn't be able to handle that kind of slick surface. But on a dry, sunny day like today? Yeah, this was perfect!

Every turn, he felt her arms tighten around his waist, her hands flat against his stomach. It was both heaven and hell. He wanted to pull off to the side of the road, drag her into the forest and make love to her. Instead, he pushed the bike harder, turning into the curves and reveling in the power of the engine. Riding a bike wasn't like driving a car. It was a more sensory adventure. It was wind and curves and feeling the road in ways that a person just couldn't do in a car.

Having a woman like Gianna riding along with him only made the whole experience exponentially more vivid! After a while, he turned around and headed back to town. It was too much, he thought. He'd love to take her out to dinner and then bring her back to his place, make love to her until neither of them could speak. He suspected that Gianna would be an amazing lover. She was curious and excited about life, eager to explore.

But he still didn't trust her.

Once he knew her motives, maybe they could...hell, he had no idea what might happen because he couldn't figure her out. Something about her just didn't fit, wasn't right.

So he headed back to town, back to his house. She'd come over for help with a report. This little adventure hadn't been in the plan and he needed to get back to that plan.

Pulling into the driveway, he shut off the engine, gritting his teeth in anticipation of her pulling away from him. But she didn't. Her arms remained tightly wrapped around his waist. He enjoyed the warmth of her pressed against him.

"Are you okay?" he asked.

She lifted her head and pulled her arms away. "Yes!" she laughed. "Oh yes!" She dismounted gracefully. "That was amazing!"

Gianna pulled her helmet off and shook her dark hair out, fluffing it with her fingers. "Thank you!" she laughed, dancing a bit as the adrenaline seeped through her bloodstream. "Oh, I like that bike!"

He chuckled softly as he pulled his helmet off as well. "And no, I'm not going to display it in my living room," he told her, answering the question she'd asked earlier.

She giggled as she wiggled out of the borrowed jacket and his eyes were immediately drawn to the deep V of her soft, yellow sweater. He hadn't noticed her sweater before, but it caused her skin to seem creamier somehow. He liked the color and the style, but he especially liked the way the material hugged her abundant breasts.

Pulling his eyes away, he stacked both helmets back up on the shelf. "Come on inside. Let's figure out the problem you ran into this morning."

He didn't glance back at Gianna, knowing that if he did, he'd pull her into his arms and kiss her. He'd rip that damn sweater off of her and find out how heavy her breasts were, how perfectly they fit into his hands.

Mystery first, fun later, he told himself.

When he opened the garage door that led into his house, he realized that Gianna was lingering by his bike, her fingers sliding longingly over the chrome.

"I'll take you for another ride soon, if you'd like."

Those dark eyes lit up and he swore under his breath. Now why the hell had he promised her that? He'd come back to the house to get their relationship back on a business footing. Promising another ride on his bike did the exact opposite!

But the bright smile that lit up her features was all the pleasure he needed.

Damn, she was breathtakingly gorgeous!

"*Fantastico!*"

His body already ached from the bike ride and now she started in with her sexy Italian? Was she doing it on purpose? Did she have any idea how much her lilting voice turned him on?

Turning away, he led the way into his home office and focused on booting up his computer. His fingers flew over the keyboard, logging into the secure system at the company headquarters.

"Yes," Gianna murmured, stepping into the room and nodding her head in satisfaction as she looked around.

"Yes?" he prompted, still focused on the screen.

"This is exactly what I pictured when I thought of your home office."

Brant looked around, noting the bare grey walls and dark trim. There was a desk and his computer with built in shelves behind him that included hidden filing cabinets. A big leather chair sat behind the desk and an upholstered chair, for guests, was tucked back in a corner because he rarely had guests. Other than that, there wasn't much to the room.

"What's wrong with my office?" he asked, dropping into the leather chair.

She shrugged and dumped her leather tote on the upholstered chair. "Nothing at all," she replied. "This office is exactly what I thought it would be like."

For some reason, Brant was certain her comment should be insulting, but for the life of him, he had no idea why. The room was functional.

"What would you change about the room?" he demanded, standing up and crossing his arms across his chest.

"Oh, I don't know," she replied, spinning slowly as she took in the room. "Color, perhaps?"

He looked at the grey walls again, confused. "Why would I add color?"

She smiled and his muscles tightened. He wanted her to smile at him like that when she was naked, he thought. Yeah, naked and....

"Color makes things interesting." She perched a hip on the edge of his desk. "Color brightens one's perspective."

"And my perspective needs brightening?" he teased.

"Absolutely! If there is anyone in this world who needs a brighter perspective, it is you!"

He had no idea what she meant by that, so he pulled up the data she'd mentioned, which was still in a report format on the server and printed it out. Better to face problems he could fix rather than the ones he didn't even understand.

"What was the issue?" he asked.

"Here," she pointed. "I can't figure this out. It isn't right, but I don't know what I did wrong when putting in that data."

Brant nodded when she explained the supply orders that had already arrived at the manufacturing facility compared to the number of bottles and packaging ordered. "See? This is no matching," she explained, pointing to the various numbers she'd calculated.

He nodded, his concern increasing. "You're right." Standing up, he pulled back because Gianna smelled…incredible. Did other women smell that good? He tried to think, but it had been too long since he'd actually been with a woman.

"Okay, let me look into this. Calculate the other issues and I'll get back to you, okay?"

Gianna nodded. "Good. I'm no crazy, then," she laughed and leaned over to…

Gianna froze. Reaching to grab the printouts caused her breast to brush up against his arm. His strong, muscular arm, she thought silently. Tilting her head, she looked up into his dark eyes. He felt it too, she realized.

Pull back! Get away from him! Her mind ordered her to pull away, but her body didn't move, her heart racing even as she told herself to step away. She felt his breath, the warmth of him. Had the room become hotter in the past few moments? Impossible!

But yes, she felt the heat increase. Perhaps it was caused by her own awareness of him as a man.

He pulled back and Gianna felt surprisingly rejected. She knew that he'd felt the same pull she did. It was there in the way he pressed his lips together and the burning in his eyes. Glancing down, she noticed that his body looked just as alive as hers felt.

Brant stood up abruptly and nodded, moving toward the window and away from her. "I'll have Gerome take a look at the factory site tomorrow. Get me the data on the marketing plan by tomorrow afternoon, okay? I want to talk with the people over at the site by Tuesday morning."

Gianna frowned, wondering what had just happened. She felt dismissed. His gaze seemed shuttered now. Closed off. Anything he might have felt a moment ago was gone, suppressed underneath the layers of control he was known for.

"Right," she muttered, leaving the report on his desk and grabbing her tote. "Tuesday. I'll have the data for you by Monday."

With as much dignity as she could muster, Gianna left the dull office. As soon as she'd rounded the corner where he could no longer see her, she increased her pace, wanting to get away from him and the complicated, swirling feelings he brought out in her. She'd made a fool of herself with a fuddy duddy. What was she thinking?

Brant Jones wasn't the man she wanted for her life. And she wasn't here in the United States to fool around. She was here to learn. She wanted the experience of working in the United States and then she'd go back to Italy to start her own business. She didn't have huge ambitions, just a small shop all her own. Or maybe a chain of small, boutique stores. She'd sell...well, she didn't know what she'd sell, but something. Something colorful and beautiful! Something that would...

A shop that she owned where stupid, boring men with too many muscles couldn't reject her!

She wiped furious tears from her eyes. It shouldn't matter. He was nothing. She had plans and a life that she wanted to build. Brant Jones was just a stepping-stone on the path to her dream!

Gianna repeated that thought all the way home. But as soon as she stepped into her tiny, cheap apartment, which she'd rented but hadn't bothered to decorate, because she hadn't planned to stay long, she burst into tears. Sitting down on the sofa, she curled into a ball, wondering why she had to be attracted to a man that didn't want her! Why Brant Jones? Of all the men in Denver, why did he have to be the one that set her senses on fire?!

No more, she promised herself. She was here for one thing, and one thing only! If she learned more about this confusing but fascinating American culture, great. If not...

She looked around at her bare apartment and sighed in disgust. "Enough!" she announced to the cold walls. "*Non piu!*"

Grabbing her purse, she headed out. Three hours later, she felt better as she unfolded a cheerful, bright comforter for her bed, added colorful pillows to the sofa, and spread around a few sparkling knick-knacks. Curtains were a bit of a problem, since she couldn't figure out how to hang them, but she'd pick up tools later this week and learn how to hang the brackets. Draping the curtains across the club chair, she hefted the box of yellow, red, and green plates and bowls into the kitchen. Stacking the dishes that had come with the furnished apartment, she stored them in one of the cabinets she wasn't using and put her new dishes onto the shelves. Then she began pulling ingredients from the fridge. Cooking! She would cook something delicious and spectacular! Cooking always made her feel better, more alive!

Chapter 4

Gianna frowned at the data, then at the other numbers. "Well, I'll...!" she stopped, not remembering the English word. She'd been slipping into Italian a lot lately. She hurriedly printed out the data in question before rushing down the long hallway.

"Is he free?" she asked Todd, pausing outside of Brant's office.

Todd opened his mouth to respond, but a deep voice echoed from the open office door. "Come in, Gianna!" he bellowed.

Gianna cringed, wondering what she'd done wrong this time.

"Someone is stealing from you," she announced, slapping the report down on the desk in front of him. She moved around to the side where he was sitting, leaning over so that she could explain. "I figured out why the data was wrong this past weekend. See these numbers? And these show someone is buying extra ingredients, only to sell them a few days later. This," she continued, pointing to a delivery truck entry, "is when the ingredients leave the warehouse. And this..." she pointed to a list of employees, "is everyone who was working on these particular days."

Gianna stopped, looking down at him to see if he understood what she was saying. But he wasn't looking at the data. He was looking up at her. And was that...she swallowed, thinking that perhaps it was admiration in his eyes. Admiration and...something more. That sizzling, powerful sensation hit her and she wasn't sure what to do with it.

Pulling back, she stepped out of his way, not sure how to handle Brant Jones. He was too confusing. Italian men, she understood.

Most American men, they looked at her breasts and she understood them. But Brant…he didn't and she didn't. And that scared her and thrilled her at the same time.

Retreat!

Stepping further back, she waved at the report. "Anyway, do with that information what you will," she announced and walked towards the door to his office. "If you need more evidence, I will cross check the list of names and come up with more."

"That's okay," he stood up. His hands slid into his pockets and he nodded down towards the reports. "This is excellent work, Gianna. I'm impressed."

She'd almost made it to the door of his office. Had she heard him correctly? Had he just complimented her?

Back in her office, she packed up for the night, wondering if she could…if maybe…

Still confused, Gianna closed her laptop and…just before she left, she remembered the secret papers she'd printed out. Turning left instead of right, she pulled the potentially embarrassing papers off of the printer. Even as her eyes moved down the page, she didn't understand what was on them. The words made absolutely no sense and the statistics…what did they mean? They were absolute gibberish!

Brant would know what they meant. But there was no way she would go to him. He would…she shuddered, thinking about the man. Nope. He could never know about this information.

She rushed down the hallway. But just before she was about to turn the corner, she stopped and looked towards Brant's office. There he was! The man stood in his doorway, his hands still in his pockets, watching her. She wondered briefly if he'd been talking to Todd. But Todd came out of another office, heading in the opposite direction.

Why was Brant just standing there? Why...why did he have to be so handsome?! And so enigmatic!

Yeah, that was one of the words she'd learned last night and as soon as she'd read the word, Gianna realized it suited Brant perfectly.

Breaking free from his gaze, Gianna realized that she was still holding the papers with the odd data in her hands and quickly stuffed them into her tote so that he wouldn't suspect what she was doing. With a guilty glance in his direction, she hurried towards the elevators. As she reached out, Gianna noticed that her finger shook and she pulled her hand back, glancing around to make sure no one else had noticed. There were several other staff members around her, but they were focused on their phones or their conversations. Several of them smiled at her and two of the ladies included her in their conversation while everyone waited for the elevator to arrive. But as Gianna unlocked her car, she had absolutely no recollection of the conversation at all. She might have agreed to sell her first born child or just a lunch date.

Chapter 5

By the time she'd cooked a healthy dinner of chicken and vegetables sautéed in a delicious red wine sauce, Gianna decided that she wasn't hungry for dinner. So instead of sitting down to eat, she shoved everything into the fridge and focused on the issues she'd discovered today. Was there more to the stolen items than what she'd found? And why had Brant looked at her like that last night? That confusion caused her stomach to rebel so badly that she'd convinced herself that it hadn't been admiration in his eyes. It had been amusement. Brant Jones thought she was silly! He thought that she'd misunderstood the data that she'd brought to him!

After a restless night, she woke up and glared at the blank ceiling, her mind whirling with ideas. In the early morning light, Gianna's determination settled in and she pressed her lips together.

"I'll prove it to him," she vowed and threw the pretty, yellow sheets off, stomping into the bathroom. Showering and dressing in a bright red dress then adding a pair of killer black heels, she fluffed her curls and let them air dry while adding a touch of makeup.

Picking up her phone, she sent a text message to Brant. "Have an appointment. Will be in late today." She smiled, thinking that he'd assume that meant a lady doctor appointment. Oh, it was glorious to be vague!

With that done, she grabbed her bag and computer and headed out. She'd prove to Brant that someone was stealing from the company and then he'd have to take her seriously!

GPS was a splendid invention, she thought as she pulled into the warehouse facility an hour later. Since she'd been heading out of town and away from downtown Denver, the drive had actually been relatively nice. Perhaps it had been the anticipation of seeing the look in Brant's eyes that he couldn't deny her evidence, which had made the drive so much more pleasant, but Gianna didn't analyze her feelings too closely.

"Good morning," she cheerfully greeted the man standing at the front desk. He was a relatively big man with a blue uniform shirt and matching pants, carrying an official looking clipboard.

"How can I help you, little lady?" he drawled, smiling down at her.

Ignoring his patronizing tone and belittling words, she smiled tightly. Oh, how she wished she was tall and intimidating! "I work at the headquarters building for Brant Jones," she explained, lifting her badge so he could see her picture. "I was working over the weekend, and noticed a discrepancy in the numbers, but he didn't agree with me. So, I thought I'd prove it." She tilted her head, playing on his belief in women being inferior. If it proved he was a thief, she'd laugh as he was hauled away in handcuffs. It would teach him not to underestimate women! "You don't mind, do you? I mean," she leaned forward slightly, as if telling him a secret, "he's such an old stick in the mud, wouldn't it be nice to prove him wrong? Just once?"

The man laughed and nodded. "Hell yes! Thankfully, I like Mr. Brant. He's a great boss, but so far, he's never been wrong." He gestured toward her file filled tote bag. "What's this about? Maybe I can help you."

She sighed. "I told him there are…" she paused and pulled the reports out of her bag, pretending to look at her numbers even though she knew exactly what she was looking for and where the ingredients were stored. Tapping her pencil against the list, she nodded before continuing. "I said there are forty-five of the glycerin bottles that have broken over the past month. He says that only thirty were broken."

The man's eyebrows drew closer. "Glycerin bottles? We haven't broken any of them."

She blinked, her eyes wide as she pretended to be startled. "Really? Then we're *both* wrong?"

He laughed, waving his clipboard towards the door. "Come on back, honey. I'll let you count them yourself."

Exactly what she'd been hoping for, Gianna thought in satisfaction, practically dancing as she followed the man down the long lines of stacked ingredients and products ready to be shipped out. Everything came through this facility, then went back out to be mixed in the production rooms, then back here as a final product and sent out to retail sites. So if anything was happening, it was happening here.

As the big guy walked her through the aisles lined with the tall, metal shelves, several other workers called out to each other, laughing or joking as they went about their business. "It's very different here than at the headquarters office," she commented, looking around, her eyes wide and filled with wonder.

"Yeah, I think this is a better place to work than the stuffy offices where you go every day." He looked down at her and winked. "Any time you want to come out here, I'll find a place for ya, honey."

Gianna smiled, but inside, she cringed, horrified at the thought of working with this man. Then something else occurred to her. There were no women out here. None! There were women all over at the headquarters offices. What was going on with the hiring process out here? Did women just not want to work in a warehouse? Interesting mystery and a conundrum she'd bring up with Brant once she got back to the office.

"Hey Joe! Those go over on aisle fifty. Not here!"

Joe was working a forklift, which was carrying what looked like heavy boxes, but could be packed with cotton balls for all she knew. In fact, everyone around here seemed to be working hard.

Joe called out something else and Gianna knew that this was her opportunity. "Why don't you go tell Joe where he should put that? I know I'm a burden, but I just want to prove Mr. Jones wrong and my information right." She pointed to her report where she'd circled the aisle that contained glycerin. It wasn't the aisle she would be going to, but it looked accurate enough.

The man looked at the number, then back at the forklift operator and nodded his head. "Yeah. I'd better go fix this mess before something gets lost." He waved his clipboard over towards the aisle in question. "Go ahead and do your count. I'll be right back."

Gianna waited until he walked towards Joe, still yelling, before she hurried to the aisle in question. Pulling out her phone, she started snapping pictures. The glycerin was in one place, but she was three rows over, the exact place where...there was nothing. Nothing at all! Staring, she glanced at her report, then at the number over the huge, metal shelf. This was the right place, but there wasn't anything here! What in the world?!

"Hey! What the hell are you doing over here?" the big guy called out, hurrying towards her. Gianna quickly, and as surreptitiously as possible, snapped some pictures of the empty spot, and then turned and beamed innocently up at her escort. "I think I have what I need," she told him. "I'll head on out now.'

"What the hell is going on here?" he demanded, grabbing her arm and pulling her back. "You're not here to check on glycerin, are you?"

"I am!" she told him, gasping at the pain from his grip. "Let me go!"

"Not a chance, little lady. You're a spy, aren't ye?"

She yanked at her arm, but his hand was holding her so tightly, that her attempts were only hurting her further. "Stop it! Let me go!"

The man bent down low, snarling in her face. "You're a handful of trouble, aren't you, girlie?" He snickered. "You know what we do with bad baggage around here?"

Gianna was terrified but didn't want to show it. Reaching into her jacket, she pressed the button on her phone, ready to record the conversation. She couldn't see the button, so she hoped it was the right one. With her luck, she'd probably pressed the video button and was taking a video of the inside of her pocket. Going with hope and probably a huge dose of stupidity, she lifted her chin, glaring at the man. "You're a thief! You're stealing supplies from the company that pays you!"

The man's hand tightened on her arm. "What do you know about money? You're just a pretty little toy that's probably only good for one thing. Did the big guy send you? Are you the bait that's going to get me and my crew to confess?" He squeezed her arm harder. "You're pretty enough, I'll give you that. But you gotta have brains to get anything out of me."

Gianna was furious now. "Why would you do it? Why steal supplies? They aren't worth enough to keep you out of prison."

"You don't know anything. You have no idea how much this company makes. Selling a bit on the side gives me enough to go on nice vacations, just like the big guys in the city get to do."

Gianna didn't think he would care that she didn't take extravagant vacations. "I think you should return all of the supplies, sir. This is a good company. Brant and Reid pay you a good salary."

He stared at her for a moment of stunned silence, then threw back his head laughing. "You think I give a shit what the guys up in the big building want?" He turned and shoved the clipboard onto a shelf. "They make more than enough. Time for them to share a bit of the good stuff."

"Hey Tony!" someone called out from the main aisle.

"I'm busy! Whatever it is, handle it!" he roared.

There was a long silence and Gianna knew that she had to act fast. This man wasn't just angry, he was mean. Since he was in charge of shipping, Gianna was very aware that she could be at the bottom of a box being shipped to somewhere she couldn't pronounce if she didn't act soon.

"Tony, so that's your name. Why don't you let me go and I'll just walk out of here and keep my mouth shut?" she lied, smiling prettily up at him. "I'm just a little girlie, like you said. Who is going to believe me anyway?"

He licked his lips as his beady eyes roved over her figure. "Yeah, you're a little thing, but you got all the right parts in the right places. Maye we'll have just a bit of fun before we get rid of your cute ass."

Uh oh. Gianna didn't like the sound of that. She might have gotten herself in a bit deeper than she had anticipated. Time for action, she told herself.

Slumping over a bit, she curled her shoulders inward, trying to make him think she was defeated. "I'm sorry, Tony. I just..." she waited a moment, added in a dramatic sniff for effect. She felt his hand loosen slightly and knew that the moment was right. Moving closer, she looked up into his eyes, a single tear sliding down her cheek. "Tony, please. I'm sure we could figure out a way to resolve this." As his mouth curled into a disgusting smirk, she put her hands on his arm for leverage. With all of her might, she pulled her knee back and...she saw the exact moment he realized what she was going to do. It was a split second of recognition. Thankfully, she had momentum on her side and her timing was perfect. He didn't have a chance to block her attack. Her knee slammed directly into his groin. Gianna followed up by swinging around, using her body's momentum to slam her elbow into his nose.

She was just about to hit him again when a steel arm wrapped around her waist, lifting her off her feet.

"Hold on, tiger," Brant's voice whispered softly in her ear as he carried her out of the area and police officers swarmed in to handcuff Tony.

Gianna peered around Brant's broad shoulders, her heart pounding wildly as she realized how close she'd come to being in serious trouble.

Brant set her down, holding her steady for a moment until she looked up at him.

"Are you okay?" he asked gently.

Was she okay? Gianna wasn't sure. She was shaking like a leaf, and her elbow hurt a bit. "I think so," she temporized. That was becoming a habit today, she told herself.

"What are you doing here?" he asked.

Gianna pulled away, ducking under his arm and stepping around him.

But he intercepted her, stepping in front of her. "Gianna, look at me!" he ordered.

She stopped and frowned up at Brant, peering around him to watch the police lead several others out of the warehouse. How had he figured out who else had been in on the thefts? Darn it, he'd been better than she was! Smarter and faster and...well, he hadn't put himself in danger.

Knowing she'd done something stupid, she retreated to what she knew best. Focusing back on him and his angry expression, she went on the defensive. "You didn't believe me when I told you that someone was stealing from you yesterday, Brant!" she announced, throwing her hands up in the air. "You didn't believe me and you've been giving me silly, pointless assignments until this one. Finally, you give me something real and when I find something that I know is true, you no believe me!"

"I believed you, Gianna!" he growled. "Why did you come out here to confront the man?"

He believed her? She'd been about to begin her second argument but...well, she hadn't figured out what her next argument was going to be...he *believed* her?

He was still glaring at her and she didn't like it. "Because I needed proof! The way you looked yesterday, you...well, I wasn't sure you'd believed me initially, so I'd convinced myself that you didn't believe me, and I had to prove it to you."

Brant wasn't sure if he was more furious with her or with himself. Probably her, he thought, wanting to spank her pretty butt! "You had to prove *what* to me?" he roared, matching her anger now.

Brant looked down at her, his anger increasing as it hit him just how much danger she'd been in. And it was his fault because he hadn't confided in her, hadn't included her in his plans to investigate and find the culprits after she'd brought him the data proving her point yesterday.

"You shouldn't have come out here by yourself!" he snapped. "You should have trusted me! You should have..."

"As you trusted me?"

"Yes!"

"You didn't say anything when I gave you the information yesterday! Not one word!" Her passionate Italian nature was rearing its beautiful head and he liked it. Too much!

"Gianna! You wore heels to confront a thief. What the hell were you thinking?"

Her shoulders trembled as her indignation increased. "What I'm wearing has no bearing on this conversation!"

They were yelling at each other now, completely unaware of everyone around them. Thankfully, the other warehouse employees were more interested in watching their supervisors being walked to the waiting police car in handcuffs.

"Of course it does! What if you'd needed to run away? What if you'd needed to do something other than slam the guy's testicles into his throat? Huh? Did you think about that before coming out here?"

"I hadn't intended to confront the man! I was just going to take pictures and bring them back to you, then demand that you do something to stop the thief!"

"Good plan! But that doesn't help the fact that you were confronted. And even after you were confronted, you didn't say or do anything to get yourself out of the situation and back to a safe position! Damn it, Gianna! You put yourself in danger!"

And with that, he moved away from her, running a frustrated hand through his thick hair. Swinging back to her, he pointed his finger right at her. "Don't you *ever* put yourself in danger like that again!" he growled, so furious, he could barely get the words out. Pacing back and forth again, his mind going over and over how he'd found her. She'd been about to...she'd almost been hurt!

She opened her mouth, once again ready to argue with him. But this time, he'd had enough! He couldn't handle watching her full lips spout dangerous words while she bristled with emotion.

Or maybe it was just all the adrenaline pumping through his body. He didn't care. He pulled her into his arms and kissed her.

He'd only intended to kiss her so she couldn't argue with him any longer, but as soon as his lips touched hers, the fire that had been sizzling between them for the past several months exploded into a bonfire! The heat and fear, the incessant desire for her all comingled into a white hot need. He nibbled her lower lip until she opened for him. As soon as her lips parted, his tongue moved inside, teasing and taunting hers. Her long, sexy fingers dove into his hair, pulling him lower as she pressed all of those incredible curves against him. That only inflamed him further until he didn't care that they were in a warehouse or that he didn't trust her. At this moment, with her body against his, fitting against the hard planes of his body so perfectly, his mind stopped functioning.

A quiet cough pulled Brant out of the haze of lust. Slowly, almost painfully, he lifted his head. For a long, breathless moment, they stared into each other's eyes. He watched as her tongue darted out, licking swollen lips and he wanted to roar with frustration and need!

"Don't do that," he groaned, leaning into her but closed his eyes when she shifted against his erection, cradling and rubbing against him. Damn, she felt good! Better than good.

"Sorry to bother you, Mr. Jones," a tentative voice said, accompanied by a throat clearing.

Painfully, he pulled back, lowering Gianna down to the floor. Turning and suppressing his need to punch out whoever had interrupted them, he found one of the police detectives looking away as if that could give him and Gianna a bit of privacy.

"What's up?" Brant asked, still holding Gianna. She felt too good, too soft and feminine to release just yet. Besides, she was currently leaning heavily against his side and he wanted to pull her back around and start kissing her all over again.

"I'm sorry, Mr. Jones," the detective replied, turning to face him. "We've arrested all six of the employees and my team will move in to gather more evidence. They're all saying that they didn't steal anything, that the supplies must have been misplaced.

That's when Gianna remembered her cell phone. "*Uno momento*," she mumbled, forgetting to speak in English. Lifting her phone out of her jacket pocket, she stared at the screen. "This might help," she said and pressed the button to replay the recording. Crossing her fingers, she waited. The sound was muffled but, slowly, the conversation between herself and Tony unfolded. It wasn't an outright confession, but it was clear that Tony had stolen something.

"Does that help?"

The detective smiled, nodding his head. "That's a pretty good start," he laughed. "Can I take this for now? I'll have it returned to you as soon as the police technician downloads the information."

Gianna nodded, unaware of her dark curls teasing Brant's hand as it rested on her neck. "Of course. Please take it and I come pick it up when you're finished."

The man nodded and slipped the phone into a plastic evidence bag.

Gianna suspected that she wouldn't see her phone for a while. It might even need to be replaced.

"Thank you, Detective," Brant said, extending his hand to the man. "Your timing was perfect this morning."

"My pleasure." He looked at Gianna. "Ma'am, please let us do the tough stuff from now on. I don't like thinking what those men might have done to you if we hadn't arrived in time."

Gianna didn't answer, but thought that she'd had things well in hand at the time of his arrival. Looking over at Tony, she saw that a paramedic was cleaning up the blood from Tony's busted nose. She smiled as she looked lower, noticing the ice pack on his groin area.

"Come on, tiger," Brant urged, putting a hand on her arm and...

Hissing, Gianna pulled back.

"What's wrong?" Brant demanded. "What did...?"

He stopped when her hand moved to her upper arm. "Gianna, what the hell?"

She carefully slipped her jacket off and examined her arm. A vicious bruise was forming, turning her creamy skin dark purple. "How the hell did this happen?" Brant demanded, taking her hand and lifting her arm up gently.

The detective turned, his eyes sharpening on the bruises. "Ma'am, what happened? Did Tony Mandoli do that to you?"

Gianna shrugged, not wanting to make a big deal about the bruises. "I tried to walk away, he tried to stop me." She waved her hand slightly. "*Non e niente.*"

"Dammit Gianna! This isn't nothing!" he argued, quickly interpreting her comment. "You are going to press charges for assault."

Gianna's mouth opened up in horror. "But..." she waved her hand towards Tony who was being led to a police cruiser still holding the ice pack to his groin. The guy limped slightly and she smiled, warmed by the fact that he was just as hurt as she was. "I did that to him."

The detective moved closer. "The argument could be made that you acted in self-defense. I'm guessing that he was holding your arm first?'

"*Si.* Yes, but..."

The detective shook his head. "It's up to you, ma'am. But I'd like to add on assault charges. A bruise like that might also help the judge to deny bail. If he's a threat to society, he shouldn't be out walking the streets."

"He's right, Gianna." Turning back, he nodded to the detective. "She'll file assault charges. I'll make sure of it. I'll even drive her to the courthouse to make sure that she follows through."

Gianna frowned, fully aware that he said the last part just for her. But the detective smiled. "Good idea." With a nod to both of them, he walked away, heading towards his vehicle.

Brant pulled out his own cell phone and took pictures of the bruises on her arm.

"This isn't necessary," she argued, trying to pull her arm away.

"Hold still," he ordered, gently holding her arm in place as he snapped several more pictures. "There, that should do it. I'll have our lawyers file the charges today and we'll get an order of protection for you as well. I don't want to take any chances with that guy."

"I will handle the charges," she told him, tugging her jacket back on and looking around for her purse. Brant grabbed it and handed it to her.

"Let's go, Stallone," he took her arm more carefully this time as he led her out of the warehouse.

Chapter 6

"She tried to take on a guy twice her size!" Brant grumbled, pacing back and forth in Reid's office. "What the hell was she thinking?"

Reid chuckled and dialed a number.

"Who the hell are you calling?" Brant glared at his brother.

"Who do you think?"

Brant leaned his head back, rubbing the tense muscles. "Right. Gang up on me."

"Yo!" their youngest brother answered. "What's up in the land of Oz?"

"Get this," Reid, the oldest of the brothers began eagerly, "the woman driving Brant crazy just increased her efforts."

"Uh oh. What did the lovely Gianna do now?" Mack asked and both brothers could hear the amusement in his voice.

"How the hell do you know her name?" Brant demanded.

Reid grinned. "Selena and I went up to the mountains last weekend and I spilled to our baby bro."

"Interesting issues you have going on there," Mack teased. "So what did your lovely lady do to spark your temper this time?"

Brant glared balefully, refusing to say another word.

"Since Brant is furious, I'll fill you in."

"I'm all ears," he laughed.

Ten minutes later, Mack was no longer laughing. "Why the hell did you let her go out there to confront the bastard? That's what we're for! You should have called the police!"

Brant dropped into one of the big leather chairs in Reid's office, pouring a glass of the good scotch his brother hid in his office liquor cabinet. "I *did* call the police. That's the part Reid forgot to tell you. I showed up right as the guy was ready to do some damage. Thankfully, our timing was good and only the warehouse manager was hurt."

"And Gianna's arms," Reid filled in.

Brant closed his eyes, hating the memory of her soft skin bruised like that. "I'd better not ever see that asshole again!" he growled. "I'll kill him!"

"I didn't hear that," Mack laughed. "So how much was stolen? And what's next on your lovely lady's list of adventures?"

The idea of taking her out for another adventure on his motorcycle flashed through Brant's thoughts. But memories of their kiss lingered and he shook his head. "We're going for the boring stuff from now on," he announced. "No more adventures."

"Pity," Reid teased, his eyes sparkling over the rim of his glass. "I think you should have many more adventures with Gianna."

"Nope!" he declared firmly. "Mack, what's going on in your world?" he asked, changing the subject. He didn't want to think about this morning any longer. Their lawyer, a beautiful but deadly shark named Andrea, had already filed a restraining order and worked with the prosecutor to ensure the appropriate charges were filed.

"Change of subject," Reid announced. "You're coming for Thanksgiving," he announced to Mack. "Both of you." It wasn't a question.

"We're not doing our usual football games up here?" Mack replied.

"Selena wants a traditional Thanksgiving meal. I'm supposed to make sure both of you are there. So don't even think about missing it."

"Selena is amazing," Mack laughed. "What can I bring?"

"Anything you want. Or more specifically, anything you want to have for the meal. We'll still get plenty of football in. She promised not to mess with that."

"Good woman," Brant replied, lifting his glass in a salute.

"I'll be there. And I'll bring something. No idea what though."

"I'll be there as well," Brant agreed. "Hot wings okay?"

And both men laughed. Mack couldn't see the glare their oldest brother gave Brant, but he could assume. "You're playing with fire," Mack teased.

"I know. But is there any other way?"

All three brothers chuckled.

Chapter 7

The doorbell rang and Brant looked around. "Who the hell is visiting on Thanksgiving day?" he demanded, irritated but not sure why.

Okay, so he knew exactly why he was angry but he wasn't going to admit it to his brothers. He'd never hear the end of it if he even hinted that he wanted to be at the office. But not for the regular reasons. He wanted to be there because he wanted to see Gianna. He needed to hear her and see her. Four days without her was too long.

Besides, just because he wasn't going to see Gianna for four days, it wasn't a good enough reason to be snapping everyone's heads off! He should be relieved, he told himself. He should be happy that he'd be away from the woman, not trying to figure out her next move, or avoid making a move on her.

After that kiss at the warehouse, Brant hadn't slept well and, even when he was awake, he couldn't stop thinking about her. And dreaming about her. Aching for her!

"Damn it!" he growled and stood up, stalking away from the sofa.

"You okay?" Selena asked gently, pausing as she moved from the kitchen area to answer the door.

"I'm fine. Sorry about that."

He smiled apologetically, softening his outburst. He liked Selena a lot. She made Reid happy and that was all that mattered to him.

Reid wiped his hands off on a towel and put a hand to the small of her back. "He's just grumpy because he thinks he won't see Gianna for several days," he explained, kissing his wife on the cheek. "He'll ease up as soon as he knows."

Selena blinked, confused as she looked from her husband to Mack and then to Reid. "Did none of you tell him then?" she asked, gesturing vaguely towards the front door.

Mack laughed. "And ruin the surprise? Why would we do that?"

Selena sighed. "You brothers are truly evil," she muttered, turning to answer the doorbell. "I'm so glad I was an only child."

All three brothers chuckled, but by the time she'd disappeared, Brant's curiosity got the better of him. "What didn't either of you tell me?"

He heard the front door open and then voices. Feminine voices. He glared first at Reid and then at Mack. Then he recognized the lilting Italian accent mingled with the soft tones from Selena.

"Oh, by the way," Reid came up and draped a carefully casual arm over Brant's shoulders, "Selena invited Gianna to Thanksgiving dinner."

Mack chuckled gleefully as all three men turned to face the front of the house just as Selena walked in with Gianna.

Brant felt like he'd been punched in the gut. She was absolutely stunning with all of those soft, dark curls piled on top of her head like that. She had a few sparkly things in her hair, but he had no idea why. The sparkles just pulled his attention away from her soft, full lips. But only for a moment. All it took for him to focus back on those lips was her smile and he was lost.

"Reid, Brant, you already know Gianna, obviously. Mack, this is Gianna Lianar from Italy. This will be her first Thanksgiving, so we're going to make it extra special!"

Reid took one of the casserole dishes Gianna carried. "Welcome

Gianna. We hope this experience won't make you hate our traditional eating-fest."

Mack took the other dish. "So, *you're* Gianna," he smiled charmingly, tucking the dish under his arm. Lifting her hand to his lips, he bowed slightly. "I've heard a lot about you. I think I'm going to have to visit my brothers more often," and he kissed her fingers lightly.

"Back off," Brant warned threateningly.

Mack only peered coolly over his shoulder, trying to hand the dish to his brother. "Brant, could you put this on the counter while I get our guest a drink?"

Brant ignored the casserole dish and took Gianna's hand. "*I'll* get the lady a drink. You take care of that dish."

Leading Gianna over to the table where Selena had set out wine glasses and bottles of both white and red wine for dinner, he glared at his brother over Gianna's lovely head. "Ignore him. He's just an…idiot."

Gianna's soft giggle caught his attention. "What's so funny?" he asked, lifting the bottle of red.

"Your brother is quite charming," she teased. "And is he, perhaps, a bit taller than you?"

"No!" Brant snapped, pouring the wine and handing it to her. "And he's a mountain man. He hates the city, preferring to live out in the wilderness with the wild animals. Stay away from him. I don't think he's up to date on his rabies shots."

More laughter, this from everyone, including Mack who'd brought the dish over to the counter and peered underneath the foil covering. "What did you make?"

Selena swatted at his hand, then turned to Gianna. "I told you that you didn't need to bring anything. Between these guys and me, we had everything covered."

Gianna sipped her wine, holding it in front of herself

defensively. "I have read a great deal about Thanksgiving. From what I understand, everyone brings something to contribute to the meal. So I was just following the rules."

Brant ran a hand up and down her back. "There aren't any hard and fast rules about Thanksgiving. Most families just make it up as they go along and have their own personal traditions."

Selena smiled. "What did you bring?"

"Well, I don't really know how to make American foods. I've tried to cook some of your traditional dishes, such as macaroni and cheese, but everything just turns out burned or inedible. So for today, I went back to the recipes my momma or papa taught me to cook over the years. Since you said you were roasting a turkey, I brought Italian roasted vegetables and...*piccolo cannoli* for desert." She shrugged. "I know that pumpkin and apple pie are traditional, but I don't have anything similar that I know how to make."

"Sound delicious," Brant assured her.

"I agree," Reid said and started to slip his fingers under the wax paper cover to grab one of the small cannoli bites. But Selena smacked his hand. A moment later, Selena yelped, laughing when Reid picked her up and tickled her neck, nuzzling along her nape with his nose.

Gianna watched the affectionate byplay, feeling Brant's hand curl into a fist against the small of her back. Why? Did he not think that love between people was beautiful? Looking up at him, trying to understand, she couldn't interpret the expression on his handsome features. Normally, she would translate his expression to one of jealousy, but could he really have feelings for his brother's wife?

Gianna was sure that Selena would have mentioned any kind of tension between the brothers. So what was this about?

She didn't understand. These American feelings and gestures, the way Americans hid everything from the world, as if emotions were bad and should be hidden all the time…it was pointless!

"Come on in and sit down. We're watching football until the turkey is done."

Selena rolled her eyes. "Don't do it, Gianna. Come help me. Getting in the middle of those three during a football game could be dangerous."

Gianna had no idea what she meant by that, but she was relieved to be able to put a bit of space between herself and Brant. If she had her way, she would curl up on his lap and demand that he explain the rules of American football to her. Since that wasn't an option, she moved into the kitchen area, which wasn't actually a room as it was in most houses. There was just the television watching area, a large dining area and the kitchen, all of which was one massive room.

The area was nice, she thought as she set her glass of wine down on the counter. If one was cooking, the chef could still be a part of the group, not separated like in her mother's kitchen. But her mother preferred it that way, not wanting her father in the kitchen when she was cooking. They both loved to cook, so when he was in there with her, he tried to take over, which only caused bickering.

"I understand. It is a violent sport."

All three men heard her and turned as one to stare, shocked.

"What did I say?" she whispered to Selena.

Selena chuckled and topped off her glass of wine. "Don't worry about it. They just take offense at any perceived insult to their favorite sport."

Gianna and Selena moved off to another room, laughing at men and sports while the turkey cooked. A half hour later, everything was ready and Gianna helped Selena carry the various side dishes to the table.

"Over here," Brant called.

When Mack and Reid were close, he put a hand on both of their shoulders, squeezing slightly so they understood that he was serious. "Listen, whatever Gianna brought, you both are going to take a serving and eat it. I don't care if it is inedible and you are sick for the next four days, you're *not* going to hurt her feelings. Got it?"

Gianna froze in the doorway that separated the formal dining room from the kitchen, hearing Brant's warning. The brothers nodded in agreement. They were completely serious and on board with Brant's orders.

"We would never hurt her feelings, buddy," Reid assured him.

"We'll both have seconds, no matter what," Mack promised.

Selena touched Gianna's shoulder and the two women stepped back into the other room, away from the men. Gianna stood there for a long moment, not sure if she was touched because Brant was ensuring that her feelings wouldn't be hurt, or offended that he assumed she was a bad cook. She was a great cook and...oh my, what if they don't like the way she cooked? What if her seasonings were too strong? Or not strong enough?

"Stop!" Selena grabbed Gianna's hand and gave it a comforting squeeze, correctly interpreting her friend's anxious expression. "I've been to your place for dinner. You're an amazing cook! Those guys are going to love whatever is in those dishes."

Gianna smiled, but her expression was tense. "Are you sure? But if I'm good, why would Brant tell his brothers they had to eat it? Even if they get sick?"

"I'll let you know if what you brought is bad and I won't let them eat it, okay?"

She relaxed slightly, still not sure which emotion won out. "Thank you." She turned worried eyes up to her friend. "Did I bring the wrong thing? Did I mess up? I try to understand your American ways but, you are a confusing country."

Selena laughed, shaking her head. "You're putting too much emphasis on those 'rules' you mentioned earlier. Seriously, there aren't any rules." She tilted her head as she lit the candles on the table. "I suppose that some families would dictate that Thanksgiving should be foods that were served during the first Thanksgiving between the pilgrims and the Native American tribes that lived in the area. The meal is a sort of a celebration that they'd survived starvation after gathering their first harvest." She focused on lighting the last candle. "But if one were to be strict about that harvest, then no one would have mashed potatoes."

Mack stepped into the dining room, hands full of dishes, and stopped before he could put them down on the table. "What is this heresy you speak?" he demanded, glaring at his sister-in-law.

"Out of the way, shorty," Reid growled with Brant behind him, both men carrying additional bowls or plates of more food.

Mack stepped out of the way to allow his brothers to enter, turning so he could address the entire group. "Your wife just said something horrific," he announced dramatically.

Reid immediately put the sweet potatoes and sliced turkey onto the table and turned to his brother, but not before pulling Selena into the circle of his arms, nuzzling her neck slightly. "I'm sure that you just misunderstood."

"She said that mashed potatoes technically shouldn't be served at Thanksgiving."

Immediately, Reid bit her earlobe, causing Selena to gasp and try to pull away. "What is this craziness?" he demanded. "Mashed potatoes, with all of the fattening deliciousness added to them, are the whole reason to have Thanksgiving!"

Brant agreed, automatically stepping closer to Gianna, but he didn't put his arms around her. Gianna glanced up at him, wondering what it would be like to have the kind of love that Selena and Reid shared. They were so sweet together, so kind and generous with their affection. Her family was loud and raucous and her parents' home filled with love and hugs, but somehow, the affection between those two seemed different.

"I thought the primary dish was turkey?" She looked perplexedly at the pitying glances from everyone else. "What? In all of the pictures I've studied about this holiday, the turkey is always the centerpiece. In those silly commercials, the wife brings out the turkey, which is surrounded by all the pretty things on the side, and everyone ahhhs and ohhs about how beautiful and golden it is and then the man slices the turkey. Then apparently the fighting starts and everyone's feelings are hurt, someone says something bad during the meal and everyone gets drunk, everyone falls asleep afterward and leaves hours later feeling too full."

There was astonished silence after that recitation of her understanding of this day, then everyone burst out laughing.

Gianna turned to Brant, not sure she comprehended the joke. "What is funny?" she asked, her accent thickening as she tried to grasp the issue. Had she said something wrong?

The comforting arm across her shoulders soothed her wounded feelings and she looked up at Brant, hoping he didn't realize how much she enjoyed his touch.

"What? What did I say that is wrong?"

"Absolutely nothing, honey," Brant instantly replied. "You pretty much nailed it. For some reason, families all get together for Thanksgiving, even though they can't stand each other. It's an odd celebration of food and alcohol, as well as old wounds and childhood resentments. Not a great combination."

She blinked, looking at the beautiful table filled with delicious foods. "Then why do you do this?"

"It's all part of the tradition," he explained. He then turned to Selena. "What's this craziness about no potatoes? Mashed potatoes are a tradition."

Selena rolled her eyes. "I was only explaining to Gianna that roasted vegetables and Italian dessert aren't traditional, but that is okay."

"Of course it's okay! And I'm sure they are going to be delicious."

Gianna didn't see the warning look that Brant sent to his brothers, but she noticed the reactions from the two other men and had to lift her hand to hide her amusement when they rolled their eyes simultaneously.

"Sit!" Reid ordered. And everyone chuckled as they pulled out the chairs and took a seat. "To family and friends gathered round," he toasted, lifting his glass in the air.

Everyone else raised their glasses as well, and took a moment to sip the excellent wine.

Selena shared a blessing for the meal, and then everyone started passing the food around.

"Selena, what did you mean about not having mashed potatoes at Thanksgiving?" Mack asked, dumping a large portion of the fluffy, cheesy, creamy potatoes onto his plate.

She shrugged as she spooned the roasted vegetables onto hers. "Like I said, Gianna was worried that she'd done something wrong by bringing roasted vegetables and cannoli. But I realized that, if we were to stick to what was available when the pilgrims sat down for the first Thanksgiving, then we shouldn't have potatoes."

"I can't imagine Thanksgiving without potatoes," Brant added a heaping serving of the roasted vegetables to his plate. "They are the quintessential side dish."

"Yes, but they weren't indigenous to North America. So, they wouldn't have been at the first Thanksgiving."

Everyone paused with that announcement.

"Seriously," Selena continued when the stunned silence continued. "They were originally found in South American. The first Thanksgiving was back in the sixteen hundreds. Potatoes didn't come to North America until, I think, the seventeen hundreds."

Brant took the potatoes and dumped some on his plate. "Good point. Pass the gravy."

They all laughed and added more food to their plates. Selena's was the only one that seemed to have healthy portions, but Gianna knew that Selena had a history of an eating disorder so she watched what she ate carefully, never letting herself eat too much or too little. Her relationship with food was a lifetime battle.

As the meal progressed, Gianna sat back and watched, amazed at the way the three brothers teased each other. She had two older brothers, but they were much older. She didn't have the same kind of relationship that these men had with each other.

"Don't you have a younger sister?" she whispered to Brant.

"Yes, Giselle. But she's married to some prince in another country. She'll be here for Christmas, but she can't come back for every holiday like she used to. She's happy, so we allow her to stay away."

Mack and Reid both heard the comment. "I'd love to see Giselle's reaction to you saying that we 'allow' her to do anything," Mack snickered.

Reid laughed. "I think I'll tell her you said that, just for the entertainment value."

Brant rolled his eyes. "She only *thinks* she can take us on."

"Really? Do you remember who she is married to?" Mack added in. He looked at Gianna. "It used to be fun to torment our little sister. But then she went and married a huge brute of a guy. We don't mess with her nearly as much."

Reid shook his head. "I could take Jaffri," he announced.

Mack and Brant nodded. "I'd help. Again, just for the entertainment value."

Gianna blinked bemusedly. "You'd fight a man for entertainment?"

The three men shrugged. "Sure. Why not?"

Selena groaned. "Don't ask, Gianna. We'll never understand the male mind. It's a mystery better left undiscovered."

Reid winked at her across the table. "Ah, but you love *my* mysteries."

Gianna watched, smiling when Selena's pale skin turned a delicate pink.

When the meal ended, no one moved. The men were too stuffed and Selena enjoyed taunting them with ideas about going for a run or a bike ride.

Eventually, the men cleared the table. Gianna wasn't sure what was going on, but Selena relaxed with another glass of wine.

"I cooked, so the guys clean up."

Gianna grinned and lifted her glass of wine. "I like this arrangement! In my house, everyone seems to cook, but it is always the women who clean up after all meals. I could get used to this!" Gianna glanced up to notice Brant staring at her from the kitchen, an odd look in his eyes. Again, an odd look that she simply couldn't translate and that was frustrating.

"Yeah, well, next comes the football marathon," Selena warned. "So brace yourself." She stood up and waved. "Let's give them space and go out by the fire pit. I love sitting by the fire in the cold evenings. And besides, it will be quieter out there."

Gianna followed Selena out through a set of glass doors to a stone patio that surrounded a pool. The pool was covered now, but Gianna suspected that it would be a lovely place to sit and relax during the summer months. The pergola that covered a portion of the pool would add shade and there were several sitting areas, the furniture covered now to protect against winter weather. But it was nice and private, a retreat inside a bustling, noisy city with a large population. One could sense the industrious atmosphere just outside of the high walls, but in this area, it was calm and peaceful.

"This is lovely," Gianna sighed, settling down in a chair with deep cushions as Selena pressed a button to light the gas fire.

"I agree. I lived in a tiny apartment for years until I met Reid. When he convinced me to take the job here, I rented his guest house over there on the other side of the pool." She snorted. "I use the term 'rent' loosely because he never cashed my rent checks."

The door to the house opened at that moment and all three men walked out. "Yeah, but you love the results of my determination, don't you my dear?" he asked, setting his drink down on the side table before leaning over to lift his wife into his arms. He then sat down in the chair with her on his lap.

Brant sat next to Gianna on the love seat and Mack leaned back in the only other seat, stretching his long legs out in front of him.

"I thought you guys would be watching football," Selena commented, wrapping her arms around Reid's shoulders.

"Eh, the view out here was better," Reid told her.

Mack and Brant laughed, shaking their heads as they took a long sip of their beers.

"The fire is nice," Brant agreed. "Besides, our team is losing. No point in watching when they can't even catch the ball."

Selena grinned. "Gianna, they all played college football, so they are a bit particular about the way the new guys play. Being around them during a game is a bit like being around a bunch of over-opinionated critics."

"Yeah, but we're very kind in our critique of the freshman."

She laughed, shaking her head. "No you're not."

The conversation turned to a debate about the current college teams, their chances of winning the state championship, then on to Denver's professional football team. That got worse as the men hotly debated the chances of the Denver Broncos making it to the playoffs. And that debate morphed to the national hockey league and pros and cons of all of the players.

Gianna listened avidly, trying to understand the jargon. But things like "tight end" and "defensive backs" were difficult since the context of their conversation didn't translate into English words she knew well.

Dessert came next and, even though Gianna wasn't hungry, she tasted the pumpkin pie and the apple pie, discovering that both were amazingly delicious!

"So, what do you think of your first experience with an American Thanksgiving?" Brant asked as he walked Gianna to the door after she insisted on leaving. The sports debates continued, but after all of the heavy food and the two glasses of wine, she wanted to curl up and fall asleep. At least that part of Thanksgiving description was accurate, she thought.

"I am surprised that pumpkin pie is so delicious!" she admitted, feeling as if they were in a cocoon of their own. While the others argued in the other room, she and Brant conversed quietly and she enjoyed the feeling of intimacy. "I read some of the recipes and they did not sound very tempting. But the reality is fantastic!" she replied, realizing that her accent was deepening as her nervousness increased.

"Yeah, pumpkin pie one of my favorites."

Gianna stood there by the door, feeling awkward and not sure what to do.

"You shouldn't kiss me," she blurted.

He smiled slightly, but didn't move back. "I know that I shouldn't. But I think I might anyway."

Gianna's breath caught in her throat and her eyes dropped to his mouth. "The last time was too dangerous."

He chuckled and moved closer. "I've never heard the word 'dangerous' used to describe a kiss before."

For some reason, her hands lifted, resting on his chest. Had he moved closer? Gianna didn't remember him being close enough for her to touch. Not this easily, at least.

"At the warehouse, the kiss...it became out of control."

"Yeah. It kind of did."

Then he was kissing her. And Gianna kissed him back. Her hands slid up arms, holding onto his shoulders as she pressed herself more tightly against him. The sparks she'd felt at the warehouse were nothing compared to the explosion she experienced now. She felt as if her body was on fire, her breasts aching for his touch. Even as she thought it, his hands moved lower, cupping her bottom as he twisted their bodies around so that he could lift her up, using the heavy wooden door as leverage.

There was a loud noise and Brant jerked back. Both of them stared at each other, breathing heavily but neither of them moved for a long moment.

"Yeah, that was dangerous," he finally agreed.

The voices from the kitchen were the only reason he pulled back enough for her to stand on her own. Reaching down, she grabbed her purse and nodded. "Yes. We shouldn't do that again." She reached for the door, but paused long enough to look up at him, at his lips and his shoulders and...

"If you don't leave now, then I'm going to leave with you, but we won't be heading to your place."

And still, she hesitated. But when he stepped forward, she jerked and nodded. "I'm going," she announced, then slipped out the door, pulling it firmly closed behind her. She paused only long enough to close her eyes for a moment and tell herself that the man's kisses were dangerous and not right for her. And she had a plan. A plan that made falling for a man a bad idea. A really bad idea!

She kept telling herself that the whole drive home, frustrated with herself for not believing it.

Chapter 8

Brant took the stairs two at a time, telling himself that this was a bad idea. What the hell was he doing? Gianna was beautiful and sexy but...he still didn't trust her. What had she been hiding the other day under the stack of files? It had been a list of numbers and text, so had she run a report that she didn't understand? If that was the case, why hadn't she come to him for help?

Or was it something more sinister?

Perhaps he'd find out today, he thought as he took the stairs two at a time up to her apartment.

So if this was just an investigation into whatever the woman was hiding, why was he so eager to see her again?

The smile that greeted him as soon as she opened her door just about floored him. Was she always this ready with a smile for unexpected visitors? Whenever he walked into a room at the office, Gianna glared at him as if she wanted to hurt him.

"Good morning," he greeted her, smiling and looking down at her with interest.

She pulled back and her smile disappeared as quickly as it had arrived. Too bad, he thought. "Good morning, why you are doing here?" she demanded, leaning her shoulder against the door frame, her accent thick and he wanted to chuckle at her mixed up sentence structure. "We yesterday kissed and both of us comprehend that doing the kissing is a bad thing."

It *had* been an incredible kiss! "Agreed. But we're not going to do that again. "

71

She shifted slightly and he almost groaned when he realized she was wearing another soft sweater with jeans today.

"I agree with you there. So why you here now?"

"Aren't you going to invite me inside?" he teased, bracing a hand on either side of her door.

"Probably not."

He laughed and pressed his open palm against the door, pushing it wide. When she stepped back, he walked inside of her apartment and...stopped dead in his tracks.

Normally, these apartments had tan walls and matching curtains. The rental policy kept most renters from personalizing their living areas.

Not Gianna! The walls had been painted a warm, lemon yellow. The sofa was grey, but had bright green and pink pillows. There were brightly colored candles and knick knacks on most of the surfaces, but nothing looked jumbled. Just pleasantly vibrant.

He turned and saw her stuffing several pieces of paper under a book. He thought about asking about them, but from the rebellious look in her eyes, Brant figured that she wouldn't tell him. Fine, he thought. He'd figure it out eventually.

Turning his back to the colorful apartment, he nodded his head, thinking that the room was just as vital and vibrant as the woman who lived here. "You did all of this yourself?" he asked, awed by her determination and creativity.

"Yes," her chin lifted defiantly.

"It's...great! I like it."

He almost laughed when her eyes widened. "You thought I wouldn't like it?" he teased, moving closer. "It's just like you, Gianna. Colorful, vibrant, and lovely."

He watched as she bit her lower lip thoughtfully at his words, completely distracted from the purpose for his visit. "If you keep doing that, I'm going to take it as an invitation."

"Doing what?" she asked breathlessly. He felt it too, but he was trying to fight it. And even as he thought that, he looked over her head and found exactly what he was looking for. The notebook was spread out and all of those papers with the numbers and text that he'd seen on her desk were spread out.

Stepping around her, he walked over to the coffee table and looked down.

"What are you doing?" she demanded, rushing around him, trying to stop him from picking up the papers. "Those are private," she snapped, bending over to gather them together.

Brant ignored her protests and lifted one of the pages. Confused, he read the words out loud, trying to understand what she was hiding from him. But...it wasn't company data or corporate secrets. "A tight end isn't..." he laughed, shaking his head as relief surged through him. "Is this what you've been hiding for the past several weeks, honey? You were trying to understand football?"

Gianna snapped the paper out of his hand. "Yes. Your American football is so confusing but everyone seems to watch it and talk about it." He knew she was truly upset because her accent deepened to the point he had to concentrate on her words. "On Monday mornings, in the kitchen at work or before any meeting, everyone wants to discuss football and scores and quarterback misses or something. I cannot participate because I have no understanding. It is confusing and...well, the words don't make sense." She huffed, putting all of the papers on her kitchen table before turning back to face him.

Brant looked down at her, noticing again her soft sweater and the jeans. Damn, she looked good! Like a colorful butterfly!

"You want to understand football?" he asked softly.

"*Si!*" she huffed. "And I will. It is just taking me longer than I'd thought."

He chuckled, shaking his head. "Okay, change of plans. Come

with me," he ordered, but didn't think she'd follow him so he took her hand and tugged her out the door.

"Where are you taking me?" she asked, grabbing her purse and keys from the counter as she was dragged by. "And why would I want to go with you?"

He stopped and looked down at her. His plan this morning had been to talk to her and figure out what was going on between them. After yesterday's kiss and the one at the warehouse, they needed to work out a plan. But looking down at her, seeing the vulnerability in her eyes, he wanted to pull her into his arms and hold her, assure her that there was nothing wrong with her, even though she didn't understand football. But different words came out of his mouth. "You want to go with me because you like me. And you want to come with me because I'm going to teach you about football."

She pulled back slightly. "Yes, well, why can't you teach me here?"

He looked over her shoulder at the small television, shaking his head. "You don't have the right tools."

Gianna looked back at her television, a perfectly adequate television in her mind, not sure what he meant by the "right tools". But this time when he tugged at her hand, she followed behind him, anxious and worried, but eager.

When they were both in his car, he backed out of the parking spot and shifted the vehicle into gear. "Okay, tell me what you already understand about football," he ordered as he turned right out of her apartment's parking lot.

"Oh, I understand a lot about football," she teased, a mischievous smile playing at her lips. "It is played with a round ball and I am one hundred percent sure that Roma will be in the finals this year," she announced with a firm nod for emphasis.

Brant chuckled, keeping his eyes on the traffic as he shifted through the intersection towards his house. "You're talking about soccer, love. I'm talking *football*. There is a difference."

Another wave of her pretty hand in the air. Damn, he was really starting to love that gesture! It was so authentically "Gianna" and he thought it was adorable.

"Yes, you Americans call it the wrong sport. I don't know why you think to call it soccer when everyone else in the world calls it football. You are a stubborn lot, all of you."

He laughed and turned right, then left again. "I know that Europeans think that we're stubborn or self-centered. I would argue that Americans are independent."

A toss of her head caused her dark curls to dance. "You can wrap up your words in pretty phrases but the result is the same. Besides, we are not here to argue about football. This is about American football. So please...tutor me in your knowledge."

"There are consequences for sassiness," he growled as he turned left again and headed towards a residential area. But instead of pulling into a driveway, he turned into a grocery store first.

"Why are we here?"

He shut off the engine and turned to her. "If you're going to learn about *American* football," he said, emphasizing the adjective, "then you're going to learn it right. And that means, we need the right tools to enjoy the game."

He stepped out of the vehicle and came around the car, but Gianna was already out of the car before he could open the door for her. "You keep referring to these tools. I didn't think a hammer and saw were necessary to watch American football."

He put a hand to the small of her back and led her towards the entrance to the grocery store. "I see you are still limiting your vision, my dear. Tools can be a variety of things, and should never be limited to something one would use in construction." Going down the produce aisle, he tossed tomatoes, an onion, and several jalapenos into the cart. "Expand your understanding of tools and you will be a happier person."

Gianna thought he was adorable, in a rough, manly sort of way. But what he had in mind with all of the ingredients, she simply couldn't fathom. "You need chips to watch a football game?"

"Oh, yes!"

And then he steered the cart towards the beer and wine aisle. "And beer."

She rolled her eyes. "Beer is not a tool," she asserted firmly, then walked over to peruse the selection of red wine because she was not going to drink beer. Not a chance! Thankfully, the grocery store had a decent assortment of wines and she quickly chose one from Italy, preferring the rich flavors of her native country over the wines from places such as California or Virginia. Although, to be fair, she hadn't given the wines from those regions much of a chance. In her mind though, loyalty was everything! So, she stuck to her beloved Italian wines.

"So you're going to be a snob, eh?" he teased, putting the bottle of wine into the cart before heading towards the checkout. "That's okay. I will permit wine instead of beer, but you'll have to accept that you won't receive the full experience with wine."

Gianna rolled her eyes, smothering a smile as she followed him through the check-out line.

And no matter how much she protested, he wouldn't allow her to pay for half of the cost of the food. In the end, she stuffed the cash in her pocket, but was determined to pay for her half of the "tools". She'd just have to be stealthy about it. Thinking about that, she smiled to herself as she followed Brant out of the grocery store.

After loading the "tools" into the trunk of his car, they drove out of the store's parking lot and, five minutes later, they pulled into his driveway. "Come on inside and I'll show you around before we start cooking for your lessons. We have a few minutes before the game starts."

She followed him in, irritated that he wouldn't allow her to carry any of the groceries, although she gave him kudos for having fabric bags instead of using the plastic ones. She had to admire a man who preserved the environment in simple ways.

"What can I do to help?" she asked, standing awkwardly in the middle of his kitchen. Looking around, she noticed that he had a beautiful kitchen with dark cabinets contrasting with the white marble countertops and every new appliance one could hope to cook with.

"You can open a beer for me and the wine glasses are over there," he said, pointing to a cabinet by the double fridge. "Then sit there and learn the correct way to make ultimate nachos."

She giggled but retrieved a beer for him, putting the open bottle near his elbow. Then she retreated to the safety of the other side of the marble counter. She poured herself a glass of wine, then sat back to watch. "Explain these nachos to me and why they are essential to the American football watching process."

He laughed but explained, "When you are watching a game, one needs to pay attention to every play, every throw, every catch. You don't want to find yourself hungry in the middle of the game and need to leave the room for a snack. That would be a catastrophe! One has to be prepared and ready for any of the exciting plays. Otherwise, you could come back and have missed something important."

Gianna wasn't buying it. "Don't they have replays?"

He glowered at her as he shook his head. "Of course, but all plays must be watched as they happen, so they can be analyzed during the replay action."

"I see."

Gianna watched as he sliced and diced, all the while, reciting the rules of the game, the positions, the various teams, and why the Denver Broncos, the team they would be watching that afternoon, was the best.

He frowned at her with a dark eyebrow raised. "If you mock, you will be punished."

She held her breath, wondering what he might consider appropriate punishment. She could think of several, and all of them included him with his arms around her as he kissed her like he had before.

There was a moment while they both stared at each other, the tension increasing. She wasn't aware of her mouth opening slightly or her body softening. But she was completely cognizant of the desire heating his gaze and the way those eyes dropped to her lips.

"We aren't doing that," she whispered, her voice caught in her throat. Oh, but she wanted him to. She wanted him to walk around to the other side of the counter, pull her into his arms, and…

He looked down, focusing on the platter in front of him.

"Now *this* is what I call the ultimate nacho platter," he announced as he slid the platter into the oven to melt the cheese. "While the oven is heating up the cheese, let's get into position so you can hear the starting lineup."

He grabbed her hand, leading her into the large, comfortable living room area. Looking around, she understood what was wrong with her apartment – at least in his mind.

"That is a *huge* television!" she gasped, gaping at the massive screen that took up a large portion of one wall.

"Of course it is," he tugged her down onto the comfy sofa. "A man is judged by the size of his television."

"That's not what I heard a man was judged by," she teased.

"Watch it," he growled and topped off her wine. "I might have to prove to you that I am at the top of the man-heap."

Settling back, he picked up the remote control and the massive television came to life. "Now..." he started in on the rules of the game, but Gianna stopped listening. The wine was relaxing the muscles in her back and the delicious scent of nachos promised to soothe her further.

When the oven timer went off, Brant retrieved the plater, setting it down on the large coffee table in front of the sofa, explaining the art of proper chip removal. "It's a bit like a food version of Jenga," referring to the game where wooden blocks were stacked up and each player had to remove one block and hope that the entire tower didn't fall down.

For the next ninety minutes, Brant explained each play, intermittently yelling at the television for a bad call by the referee or when the opposing team scored.

Gianna learned a lot. But mostly, she learned that Brant was sweet and patient, a massive football fan, and that she wanted to touch him but had no idea how.

So, by the time the game ended, she was hyper aware of the man sitting next to her. She thought about her plans, her goals in life, and wondered if it wouldn't be too bad to give in to the attraction that seemed to grow more powerful with every interaction.

Brant was tall and handsome, but he was also ethical and intelligent, funny and...well, pretty wonderful.

Why shouldn't she take advantage of her time with him? Why wouldn't she allow herself to enjoy being in his arms? Yes, she knew that the wine was lowering her inhibitions and relaxing her. But seriously, what would be the harm in enjoying a fling with Brant? At this moment, she couldn't deny that she wanted to be with him in the most basic and primal way.

Brant glanced over at Gianna, about to explain the time out strategy the head coaches were using, but there was a strange look in her eyes. A look that told him that she was no longer interested in learning about football.

A look that conveyed the same hunger he had been feeling since he'd kissed her. No, that wasn't accurate. The same hunger he'd felt since she walked into his office for the first time several months ago. He might not have acknowledged that hunger, but it was there, burning inside of him.

And at this particular moment, he couldn't remember all of the reasons why he shouldn't kiss her again. He couldn't remember why he was so wary. All he knew was that he wanted to kiss her. To touch her and feel her soft body against his.

He pulled her closer, leaning in slowly, to give her the chance to pull away, to say no if he'd mis-read the situation.

But she didn't pull away. In fact, she leaned forward, reaching out to touch his cheek, almost pulling him forward because he was too slow. She wanted to experience his touch, and she wasn't willing to do it in slow motion!

"Gianna," he groaned and his mouth covered hers. When his tongue touched hers, she gasped at the intimate contact. It was just like the last two times he'd kissed her, but so different! Gianna vaguely heard the football game and sensed the afternoon fading into darkness. But her attention focused on Brant and his strong hands as they shifted, lifting her onto his lap so that he could deepen the kiss. Over and over, his mouth slanted over hers until she whimpered with the need for more.

His fingers shifted, sliding under her peasant blouse and setting her body on fire. Her skin felt burned, but shockingly alive as his hands explored her back and waist. When she felt his fingers move higher, she bit her lip, trying to stop herself from crying out when…

"Brant!" she gasped, arching her back as his hands cupped her breasts. She loved how she felt when he touched her. His hands were firm and confident, but gentle. He slid his thumb over her already tight nipple and she couldn't stop her hips from rolling against his. Shifting around, she straddled his hips, pressing herself more firmly against him, grinding with the same rhythm as his thumbs against her nipples. She couldn't stop, the pleasure too intense.

"Please!" she groaned. When his hand started to pull away, she grabbed his hand, "More!" she pleaded holding his thumb on her nipple.

Brant thought he might just explode! She was erotic and sensuous and he wanted to give her everything she needed. Even as he watched, he could tell she was getting closer. Her hips pressed against his shaft more firmly, over and over again. And when he knew that she was right there, just at the edge, he pinched her nipple and...

It was possibly the most beautiful thing he'd ever seen. Gianna climaxed against him just like that, throwing her head back. Her fingers in his hair held him in place as her movements slowed and then stopped, collapsing against him with her face buried against his neck.

"Damn, you're going to have to do that again for me," he groaned as he stood up with her in his arms. He struggled to walk as he carried her up the stairs. Not because of her weight, but because he was so turned on!

"*Grazie*," she sighed. He almost dropped her when she pressed a kiss to his neck. Her fingers came alive after that and he stopped, pressing her against the wall outside of his bedroom because he just had to kiss her again. As his tongue invaded her mouth, doing what his body wanted to do, he felt her fingers in his hair, tightening and then sliding against his neck.

For several long moments, they stayed just like that but it wasn't enough. Not even close!

With an almost painful groan, he pulled away and finished the walk to his bedroom. "Now, let's do that again," he announced, then hissed when she slid down his body so that she was standing. The movement against his agonizingly aroused body was both delicious and painful.

Gianna slid her fingers under his shirt. Exploring his stomach was even better than he imagined. Reaching behind him, he pulled his shirt off, dumping it on the floor. He was just about to do the same for her, but her fingers moved higher, just grazing his nipples and the touch was like an electric current connecting to his erection.

"Gianna!" he roared, grabbing her wrists and pulling them away. Shaking his head to clear away some of the lust, he backed her up so that the backs of her legs were against the bed. "No more. I can't handle it, honey. Later." Much later, he thought as he pulled her soft, sexy sweater up and over her head. He was trying to be more careful with her sweater than he'd been with his shirt, but he made the mistake of glancing down at her breasts. The lush mounds were barely concealed by the black lace of her bra. In fact, the points of her nipples looked like they might just pop out over the edge. The sweater was forgotten as he lifted her up again, taking the nipple into his mouth as his tongue lashed against the peak over and over again. It was like a ripe berry that he couldn't get enough of. Laying her down against the mattress, he followed her. Caressing one breast, his mouth teased and tortured the other. Over and over, he teased and tormented her nipples, goaded on by the gasps and hisses Gianna made.

When she pulled at his hair, only then did he relent. But he wasn't finished. Not by a long shot. Standing up again, he ripped off the rest of his clothes, tossing his jeans and boxers off to the side before reaching up to unzip her jeans. Her shoes were already gone, he had no idea where they'd disappeared to, nor did he care. Sliding her jeans down over her hips, her legs, her feet, he watched as more of her creamy skin was revealed to his pleasure.

"You're gorgeous, Gianna," he groaned as he kissed the soft flesh of her stomach. Kissing and exploring, finding other places on her body that caused her to make those appealing sounds again was his new mission. Well, that and heading lower, wanting to taste her body and see her climax again.

"Brant! *Ho bisogno di te!*" she screamed, shifting her hips back and forth as if taunting him with the movement.

"No Italian!" he grumbled, looking back up at her. "I can't take anymore, Gianna. Later, you can tell me everything you want me to do to you in Italian, but right now, you can't speak or I won't make it!"

She giggled and he thought that the sound wasn't much better.

With a groan, he moved even lower, gently opening her knees wider so that he could explore his goal in thorough detail. Looking at her like this, spread out, with glistening pink folds begging him for attention was so incredibly beautiful. He took a moment to savor her like this. But she shifted her hips again and that was all he could take. His mouth moved in lower, needing to taste her, needing to feel her against his tongue.

Slowly, he explored, finding all of the small places that tasted extraordinary! Sweet and tart, just like Gianna! As he licked and teased, he felt her fingers weave into his hair and he would have smiled at the gesture, but he was too intent on his mission. He wanted to taste her climax this time. He wanted to taste her pleasure on his lips. So he focused on the goal, listening to the sounds of her gasps and the way her fingers tightened in his hair as a barometer for what she was feeling. Over and over again, he teased that nub, sliding his finger into her heat and teasing her nerve endings from the inside. And before long, he felt her body tighten. When he knew she was just on the edge, he sucked on that nub, helping bring her over the edge.

Her screams of pleasure were like music, he thought, slowing his touch before moving away when her fingers loosened in his hair.

Standing up, he smiled, thinking about doing that again. For the moment though, he grabbed a condom and rolled it down his length, watching her breasts as she sighed in the aftermath of her orgasm.

Leaning over her, he braced his arms on either side of her head. "Ready to do that again?" he asked, kissing her neck and her breasts, waiting until she was back with him.

"No more," she whispered. "All for you."

He tilted his head, peering at her as if she'd said something insane. And yeah, he wanted to explain that the next step wasn't just for him, but he would show her instead.

Lifting her leg so that she could wrap her legs around his waist, he eased into her. She was so damn tight and slick and he closed his eyes, controlling the need to press into her more swiftly. She was wet and ready, but he felt her shift against him, her body adjusting to his invasion. When he was fully inside of her, he felt her sigh and both of her legs tightened around his waist, encouraging him.

Slowly, he started a rhythm, moving in and out of her heat, watching her features for signs that he was hurting her or that she liked something he was doing. He wanted to laugh when her eyes popped open in surprise, but he could barely think, much less laugh. All of his energy had to be focused on pleasuring her one more time. Shifting, thrusting, moving against her heat until....

"Yes!" She screamed, her fingers tightening on his shoulders as her body released one more time, her inner muscles convulsing and...

Brant wanted to savor the sensations longer but feeling her like this, plus her body thrashing back and forth pulled him over the edge. His own climax poured through him and he thrust faster and faster as the pleasure hit him hard. Harder than anything he'd ever experienced.

And when it was over, he collapsed against her, breathing heavily as he tried to catch his breath.

A long time later, he realized that her fingers were teasing his neck. And he was crushing her!

"Sorry!" he groaned as he lifted his weight off of her.

"I like it," she beamed up at him.

They were still intimately connected and he groaned as he pulled out of her. "I'll be right back."

He hurried into the bathroom to dispose of the condom, and clean up a bit before coming back into the bedroom.

"What the hell are you doing?" he demanded, stepping back into the bedroom.

Gianna swung around, clutching her jeans and her sweater in front of her. That still left a lot of skin showing and he enjoyed the unhindered view of her long, sexy legs. For a short woman, she had incredible legs!

"I..." she stammered, looking around frantically. "Americans...," her accent was thick and he suspected that a blush stained her cheeks. But in the darkness, he couldn't see her well enough.

"Yes?" he asked, walking over to her and taking her clothes out of her arms. "What about Americans?" he asked, lowering his head to kiss the sensitive skin on her neck.

"I thought that Americans had sex and then just...left."

Brant lifted his head, shocked. "Why? And who the hell told you that?" He didn't care. Instead, he lifted her into his arms, ignoring her squeak of alarm as he carried her back to his bed. "We don't leave right after sex. At least, I don't. And I don't want you to go." He paused and pulled back. "Unless you want to leave. I don't want you to do anything you're not completely comfortable with, Gianna."

Her swollen lips opened and closed, those dark, mysterious eyes staring up at him.

"I'd like you to stay," he said, his hand moving over her bare hip before curving around to her stomach. "I'd love for you to stay here all night."

The smile was slow in coming, but when it did, it blinded him even in the dark room. "I stay," she announced, her accent thick and heavy.

"Good," he replied, sliding lower. "Because I have many variations on this theme," he teased.

Chapter 9

"I think you should take the day off," Brant whispered into Gianna's ear.

Gianna smiled, stretching sore muscles. "*Non posso farlo,*" she replied, even though she really wanted to stay and have a repeat of last night.

"I love it when you speak Italian," he growled and nipped at her earlobe.

She giggled, peeking at him over her shoulder. "I didn't until last night. You never told me that you liked it."

He shifted so that Gianna was underneath him, then he pressed a leg between hers so that he was right where he wanted to be. "I love it. Unless you're yelling at me and I don't understand what you're saying."

Another giggle and Gianna wrapped her arms around his neck, lifting one of her legs so that she could rub her thigh against his hip. "Are you saying you understand me when I'm *not* yelling at you?"

He nuzzled her throat, a spot he'd discovered about midnight last night. Every time he'd touched her there she giggled. Just like now, he thought with a smile.

"It's rare that I understand what you're saying, but I don't care when you're just speaking to me. You mutter in Italian a lot," he told her.

"I do?" she asked, staring up at him innocently. "I didn't realize."

He knew she was lying. "You know exactly what you're doing.

You just don't want anyone else to know what you're saying. Are you cussing people out?"

She shrugged and he punished her for the non-answer by cupping her breast and sliding his thumb over the tip, causing her to hiss, then moan.

"Cursing is not ladylike."

He chuckled as his head slowly lowered. "That's not an answer," he replied a moment before his mouth captured her nipple.

She tried hard to keep his mouth from her nipple, but he simply grabbed her wrists and had his way. She relaxed into his hands, enjoying the way he took charge. But that was before the heat whipped through her and she shifted against him.

"Brant, I don't think..."

"I think you should call in sick today."

"I can't."

"Why not?"

She waited a moment, pulling her hands free so that she could hold his head for a brief moment. "Because I work for a horrible tyrant and he won't..." she yelped as he rolled over, pulling her on top and settling her on his stomach.

"Now, what was that about a tyrant?" he asked, his voice threatening but he followed up on that by lifting his hands, now free, to cup her breasts.

"No!" she whispered, shaking her head back and forth. Her hands gripped his wrists, but there was no pull to her touch. She wanted him to torment her like this. It was so amazing when he finally filled her and she found that blissful release. "No talking. *Stai zitto e fai l'amore con me.*"

"What did you say?" he demanded, his fingers tightening on her nipple and he loved watching her like this.

"I said," she whispered, "stop talking and make love to me."

He was fully on board with that. He grabbed a condom from

the nightstand and tore it open. He started to reach down to roll it on when she took it from his hands. Scooting lower, she took control of the process, but she did it slowly, her fingers trailing down his erection, then back up again. Finally, he took the condom from her and put on, then grabbed her by the waist and settled her back where he wanted her.

"Okay, now talk," he commanded. "Say something, Gianna," he groaned. "Anything at all."

She sighed, sinking onto his shaft with her eyes closed and both hands braced on his chest. "You feel wonderful," she told him in English, then yelped when he swatted her bottom. "I can talk all morning," she purred.

"Payback is a bitch," he warned. Gianna knew that she was in trouble, although she wasn't sure what he would do.

Her smile disappeared when he put one hand to her breast and the other slid down her stomach, teasing that nub between her legs.

"What you doing?" she demanded, shifting to accommodate him.

"Payback, my dear," he told her, watching her reaction as his thumb and forefinger pinched her nipple while, at the same time, his thumb rubbed on that lower nub.

The dual stimulation was too much and she gasped, her eyes closing. "Non! Too much!" she whispered.

"Move, Gianna. It will help if you move."

She followed his order, but wasn't sure how to move to alleviate some of the need. It was like a hot, tight bolt of lightning streaming through her body with his fingers in control. She lifted up, then let herself slowly lower back down. His fingers teased her with every shift, increasing the urgency to a point where she was almost panicked.

"*Di piu!*" she begged, pressing his finger against that nub. "More!"

"Take control, Gianna."

She arched her back, shifting her hips back and forth, trying to create a friction that would…

It happened faster than she would have thought possible! Within moments, she splintered apart, screaming as her climax took over. Wave after wave sent shudders through her. She wasn't even aware of Brant moving to be on top because all she could focus on was the pleasure. The seemingly never ending pleasure! Gasping, she tried to pull away, the intensity of her climax overwhelming. But Brant held on, thrusting into her again and again until he found his own release. By that point, another climax, smaller but just as potent, had overtaken her and she could barely catch her breath.

All night, the sex just kept getting better. Of course, the more they touched and talked, the more they knew how to touch each other.

Rolling to the side, he cradled her gently, running his hand through her tousled curls.

"You okay?" he asked softly.

"*Si,*" Gianna replied, curling into him a bit more.

"Still think you should go into the office?"

Gianna yawned. "*Si.*" And with that, she pulled away, and stood up, grabbing his shirt as she headed into the bathroom.

Brant watched her, sure that something was wrong, but not exactly sure what it was. Her head was bowed and she looked as if she might cry.

With that thought, his stomach tightened and he jumped out of bed to follow her.

As soon as he stepped into the bathroom, he found her leaning against the shower. "Honey, what's wrong?"

"*Niente,*" she muttered. "Nothing."

That was a bald-faced lie, he thought. Pulling her into his arms, he sighed with relief when she allowed it. Even snuggling in closer, burying her nose against his chest. "Did I hurt you?"

"No. You no hurt me, Brant," she assured him.

His shoulders sagged with relief again. "So, why are you upset?"

"Because..." he heard her sniff and pulled away, needing to see her eyes. Sure enough, tears formed and he wasn't sure what to say. "Because being with you is beautiful, Brant. I was so wrong about you. You aren't cold and heartless. You work too much, but you have moments of..." she sniffed again and pressed a kiss to his chest. "Moments of inspiration."

He squeezed her gently. "Moments of inspiration is a good thing, right?"

"*Si*," she agreed, nodding, her curls tickling his chest and chin. "*Molto buona!*"

"So, why are you upset?" he asked, turning on the water. "And why won't you take the day off and be with me?"

"Because I don't want to take advantage of you being the boss. If you found out that any other staff member called in sick for work so that they could make love, you would be furious."

He considered that for a moment, and reluctantly nodded. "True, but..."

"No!" she replied, slicing the air with her hand. "We work. We play later," she stepped into the steamy shower. Grabbing the soap, she rubbed it all over her body as he watched, entranced. It was incredible to watch, her hands moving all over her soft curves.

"You coming in?' she asked, peering over her shoulder as she rinsed.

He leaned a shoulder against the wall, shaking his head. "I think I'm going to stand her and enjoy the show."

Her eyes widened slightly, but then her lips curled up into an enticing grin. "A show that you can't do anything about until tonight," she teased, as she shampooed her hair.

She was right, he thought. Glancing at the clock on the nightstand, he knew that they'd have to hurry if they were going to make it into the office on time. But he didn't care. He wanted to watch and if that meant they were a few minutes late, so be it. It was good to be the boss, he thought.

Chapter 10

Gianna heard her phone ping, indicating that a text message had come in. She smiled, seeing Brant's name pop up on the screen.

"Hey there!"

Gianna glanced up and saw Selena standing in the doorway. Tucking her phone back under the file that lay open on her desk, she smiled welcomingly at her friend. "Hello! How are you?"

"Good," she replied, sitting down in the extra chair. "I'm going to the gym for a yoga class after work. Want to join me?"

Gianna considered the two options. Yoga with her friend would stretch her muscles and strengthen her body. But option B was to go home with Brant....

"I can't tonight," she decided with a firm nod.

"What's going on? You have a hot date?" Gianna couldn't hide the blush and Selena gasped. "You do! You're dating someone! Who?" she demanded, leaning her elbows on Gianna's desk delightedly.

Gianna opened her mouth then closed it, searching for an excuse that wasn't a lie. "I just..."

"Gianna!" Brant snapped, sticking his head through her doorway. "The reports from yesterday need to be recompiled with the new data. Will you have time tonight to re-run them?"

Gianna opened her mouth once again, not sure what to say. Reports? What reports? Then she caught the sparkle in his eyes and understood.

"Right! I'll get that data started," she replied, nodding for emphasis. Brant disappeared and Gianna shrugged apologetically at Selena. "I guess I am working late again."

Selena sighed. "You're right, that man works way too many hours and now he has you doing it too!" She stood up and huffed a bit. "*Fine.* Do the reports tonight, but tell him that you have plans tomorrow night. I'm taking you out for happy hour and you can complain about what a tyrant he is all night."

With that, Selena left in a flutter of pink and a cheerful wave.

Gianna grabbed her phone and read the message, smiling at Brant's command. "Be in the garage in five minutes."

Hurrying, she stuffed the papers into her bag, promising that she'd look at them after dinner tonight at Brant's house. Well, after dinner and making love with him. Every night this week, he'd brought her home to his house, cooked dinner with her, and then made love to her.

But it wasn't just sex. She enjoyed being with him. She loved cooking with him and teaching him to make her favorite recipes. And he showed her how to cook all of the traditional American meals that she'd burned during her first attempt. Monday night, they'd watched football and he'd tested her, "punishing" her when she got the answer wrong by kissing some part of her body. She'd failed the test that night, but had learned to love American football. Another night, after he made love to her on the counter, he'd pulled on his slacks, handed her his shirt and then carried her to the sofa to watch a movie. He'd even sat through a romantic comedy, which had endeared him to her even more.

So no. It wasn't just sex. She loved being with the man. If anyone had told her that just a few weeks ago, she would have scoffed at the possibility. Enjoy being with a man who worked so many hours?

But she'd gotten to know him. She knew that he was a passionate man about many things, such as his motorcycle and cooking, American football and...well, yes, he was very passionate about making love.

She wasn't sure if this was good or bad, but...she loved him.

Chapter 11

"Papa, you wanted to practice your English, so speak to me in English. I've learned several new words so I help you." Silence and then Gianna laughed. Suddenly, she turned serious, stiffening as she shook her head. "No Papa! I'm no ready yet!"

Brant stood outside of Gianna's office, not wanting to interrupt.

"Papa! I don't have everything I need yet! I don't have enough! I'm not ready!"

What the hell did she mean by that? Brant thought back to the early days. His chest tightened as he waited, listening for more information. What didn't she have yet?

"Yes. I'm being very careful. You know me."

Why the hell did she need to be careful? And how did that pertain to what she hadn't gotten enough of yet?

Brant wanted to burst into Gianna's office and demand an explanation. They'd been spending almost every non-business moment together for the past two weeks. Had he missed something? Was this conversation about stealing trade secrets?

He couldn't believe that of her. And yet, he *had* believed exactly that only a month ago. He'd even told Reid that he knew it was happening.

"Yes, Papa. I will. *Ti amo anchi'io!*" Brant knew that mean she "loved him too," because he'd been studying Italian phrases lately.

Brant went back to his office, trying to make sense of what he'd overheard. They were supposed to go out for dinner tonight and... he hadn't specified what they would do after dinner, but both of them knew what would happen. He'd bring her back to his place and he'd make love with her for the rest of the night, just as they'd done every night since that afternoon of watching football. Yes, there had been nights when they'd just slept, holding each other throughout the night. But by morning, they were ravenous for each other again.

Bracing his hands on the window, he tried to figure out what had gone wrong, what he'd missed. This just couldn't be happening! How could she steal secrets from his company!

But what else could she have meant? And why was she always hiding things from him? There were papers that she surreptitiously pushed under file folders or stuffed into her tote bag. When he asked about them, she dismissed them with a wave of her hand, then touched him. That's all it took, just a touch and he was effectively distracted.

"Damn it!" he groaned, pushing away from the window. "What the hell!?"

"Uh oh," Reid said, stepping into Brant's office and closing the door. "Something wrong in paradise?" he teased.

Brant glared at his brother, wishing that he could take a swing at him, just to release some of the fury that was slowly building inside of him.

"She's stealing from us!" he growled in a low, tormented voice, then ran a hand over his face because he didn't want to feel this. He didn't like feeling betrayed or used. Not by Gianna. Not when they'd finally...but if she was stealing, then they hadn't 'finally' anything.

"You told me that a while ago, but when I asked *what* she was stealing, you didn't know." Reid leaned forward. "Do you have more information now? And why now? What changed? I thought you and Gianna were...becoming closer, working things out."

Brant turned away. "I thought so too. But I just overheard her talking to her father about not having enough and not being ready or something like that."

Reid's eyes narrowed. "What didn't she have enough of?" he asked.

Brant sighed heavily. "I don't know. I...she and I have been... together a lot lately."

"I know. And until now, I thought it was great that you'd finally found someone who makes you feel like Selena makes me feel. But...if she's stealing from us, and keep in mind, just because she's having a conversation with her father doesn't mean she's guilty of corporate espionage, but if she *is*, I want her gone."

"Agree," Brant said, grinding his teeth as he looked up at the ceiling. "I just...I thought she was...different."

There was a long silence and Brant eventually glanced at his brother, prepared to see anger. But instead, he saw compassion and understanding. Something loosened slightly, his brother's support evident. And Brant never should have doubted that Reid would support him. The brothers had always been there for each other. Yes, they'd often ganged up to torture their sister, but rarely did they torture each other.

Reid put a comforting hand on Brant's shoulder. "I know that this hurts, but you've got to get to the bottom of this. If she's stealing from us, you need to find out. We need to assess the damage and put a stop to it."

"I know," Brant nodded. "I'll get the tech guys to look into the data downloads she's done over the past several months, and any online searches. That might turn up what she's been up to." He turned away and walked over to his desk. "Maybe they should go through her files and e-mail, find out if she's sent anything suspicious."

"Only the e-mails she's sent on the company server. We have

the right to search those files, but we'd need a warrant to search her personal e-mail."

Brant's eyes narrowed. "I'm not ready to take it to that level," he growled, although why he would hesitate to file criminal charges against anyone who tried to hurt the company was a mystery. He didn't care what his brother said, this wouldn't be handled by the authorities. They'd keep it private.

Reid eyed his brother for a long moment and Brant knew that a battle was being waged inside his head. But Brant was firm about this. He might change his mind if she's done irreparable harm to their company. Until he knew what he was dealing with, Brant was determined to keep this just between himself and Reid. And the tech guys, he supposed.

"Fine," Reid finally agreed. "But handle it fast. We need to know what's going on and get ahead of it."

"Agree," Brant replied, then lifted his phone to call in the head of their tech and security divisions.

A half hour later, he hung up, rubbing his neck as the tension increased, tightening the muscles along his neck and back. But there was one more thing to do. He sent a text message, letting Gianna know that he would be out of town for a while on an urgent business issue.

He should stay in town and ensure that the investigation progressed. But Brant didn't trust himself to stay in town and be near Gianna. She was just too...beautiful. Vivacious. Amazing.

And a liar, sadly.

So instead of staying in town and ignoring her, which could hurt her feelings, he grabbed his keys and headed out of the building. He congratulated himself on not stopping by her office to say goodbye, getting one more kiss. Because one kiss from Gianna was never enough.

Driving out of the building's parking garage, he cursed at the fates that had sent Gianna to him. Why the hell had he fallen for a woman who had the morals of a...

He pulled into his house and stalked inside, but the memories of Gianna lingered everywhere. That first day, her begging him to make love to her. On the sofa, his bed, outside, by the fire...there were so many places where they had made love...

He couldn't stay here! Brant walked to his closet and stuffed hiking gear into a duffel bag. He was probably forgetting something, but he didn't care. Not right now. He just needed to get out of his house, out of his bedroom. No way could he sleep in that bed tonight. Not after holding Gianna in his arms there just last night.

Hell, just this morning, he'd woken up to her kissing his chest. Moving lower, her soft kisses touched his stomach while delicate fingers wrapped around the erection that had come to life the moment he'd felt her touching him.

Brant stopped, closing his eyes against the memory of her warm mouth closing around his throbbing shaft, her tongue flicking that spot near the tip as her fingers curled around the base of him, tightening as her mouth moved over him.

Even when he'd tried to pull away from her, she'd resisted, wanting to take him all the way. But he'd been stronger and she'd laughed when he lifted her up and then pressed her back against the mattress. Damn, he loved her laugh. She was so free and open and caring. Gianna loved life and for the past few weeks, he'd thought that she loved him. When he'd pressed into her tight heat, she'd stopped laughing. Her eyes were bright, but her lips had curved into an O as he'd shifted against her. Over and over again, he'd thrust into her, feeling her body getting closer and closer to that delicious release. He'd figured out that she curled her fingers when she was about to climax, so when he felt her nails dig into his skin, he shifted once again, taking her over the edge to that blissful release.

Muttering a curse, he turned away from the bed. The sheets and comforter were neatly smoothed out now, obliterating all signs of the activities from this morning. If only he could do the same for his mind.

More curses and he hurried out of the house. His tires skidded as he hurriedly backed out of the garage and reminded himself to slow down before he hurt someone. Just because he was in a foul mood, that was no reason to destroy someone else's life.

Keeping his speed carefully under the speed limit, he drove through the relatively quiet streets of Denver until he reached the highway. And even then, he refused to press the accelerator too hard. But as soon as he left the city behind him, he pressed the accelerator and zoomed down the highway. He knew where he needed to go. What he had to do.

Thirty minutes later, he pulled into the driveway of Mack's cabin in the mountains. Obviously, Reid had called ahead because his brother stepped out of the front door onto the wide porch, a beer in each hand. Mack was still in uniform, but he'd stowed his weapon, obviously off duty at the moment.

Brant stepped up onto the porch and accepted the beer, gulping half of it before he nodded his appreciation.

"Maybe something stronger?" Mack offered.

Brant shook his head. "No need," he replied and leaned against the thick, wooden railing. "What do you know?"

Mack sat down in one of the big, comfortable chairs he'd built specifically for this porch, stretching his long legs out in front of him as he relaxed.

"You suspect your woman of stealing from the company, but you're not sure what or how."

Brant didn't acknowledge the comment, too shocked by thee

"your woman" part of that statement. Because it sounded too good. Gianna as his woman? Yeah, that would be nice. Unfortunately...! He simply stared out at the fading light as the sun slipped down below the trees.

Mack seemed to respect Brant's need for silence and just sat with him. The night enveloped the pair as Mack kept refreshing Brant's beers. Hours later, Mack stood up, put a comforting hand on Brant's shoulder as if to silently say, "I get it." And then he went inside.

Brant knew where the guest room was. He even had some clothes in the closet because he visited so often during the summer months. Mack had built this cabin with his siblings in mind and there was his room plus three others. Although Giselle hadn't been up here since her marriage to Prince Jaffri, a room remained ready for her.

Brant stayed in that chair for hours. He wasn't sure what time it was and didn't care. He didn't want to think, but the beer didn't stop the thoughts from filling his mind. Memories were hard to deal with, but he was determined to push her out. Focus on the problem, not the memories he told himself.

Around four in the morning, Brant stood up and went to the bedroom. He only took the time to take off his shoes before he stretched out on the bed, staring moodily up at the ceiling. Sleep would be good, but Brant didn't want to do that. He couldn't sleep because...hell, because he didn't want to dream about Gianna. He'd done that every night before that Sunday afternoon when they'd finally given in to their attraction. He didn't want to do it again. Dreaming would lead to yearning and...what the hell did it matter if he dreamed about her? The yearning was still inside of him. The need to hold her, to see her smile, and talk with her, hear that beautiful accent was a painful need that burned inside of him.

Several hours later, he heard Mack get up and start making

breakfast. Brant showered and changed into jeans, adding several layers but didn't bother to shave. One of the advantages of being in the mountains was not giving a damn what he looked like.

"Coffee?" Mack asked, offering a steaming mug as soon as Brant appeared in the main living area of the cabin. Just as in Brant's house in Denver, Mack had one big room that contained the kitchen, living area, and dining table, only on a slightly smaller scale. And while Brant had black cabinets and white marble countertops in his kitchen, Mack had gone with wood cabinets. In fact, the whole house was decorated with wood and dark colors. This place was a man cave on steroids, minus the television. Mack had one, but it was hidden away. He rarely watched television, preferring to be outside, walking through the woods. It didn't matter what the season, Mack was a nature guy. And God help anyone who hurt any part of his mountain or the inhabitants of his town, be it animal or human, because Mack would find that person and make their world miserable. As sheriff of the small mountain community, he took his duties seriously and the town respected him.

"Thanks," he muttered, then moved back out to the front porch. It was cold in the morning, but he didn't care. The cold woke him up as looking at the mountains eased some of the pain in his chest. Just looking out at the massive, snow covered mountains put his problem into perspective.

"Ready to talk?" Mack asked, dropping several logs onto the fire pit and lighting the kindling.

Brant gazed blankly at the mountains, wondering if he should just head up into the woods and think for a while. But freezing his butt off didn't really appeal and it wouldn't solve his problems.

"You know what the problem is," Brant said flatly.

"Only that you think Gianna is stealing from you."

Brant turned around, startled by the phrasing of the question.

Mack was back in his favorite chair, his hands wrapped around the steaming cup of coffee while the fire crackled in the stone fire pit.

"You don't think women are capable of corporate espionage?"

Mack laughed, shaking his head. "Oh, women are more than capable of things that even I can't imagine. They are amazing creatures," he replied softly. "Lovely and strong. They are capable of anything a man is, plus about a million other things."

"So, why do you ask me like that?"

Mack sighed and took a sip of his coffee. "Brant, in my line of work, I have to assess people and animals quickly in order to stay alive. I can't tell you how many times I've been confronted by human and beast alike. Being able to read their eyes, their body language, has helped me anticipate danger and avoid it." He leaned forward. "Your woman isn't a criminal. Reid mentioned that you'd heard Gianna talking on the phone and suspected that she was hiding something from you." He stared straight into Brant's eyes. "She isn't doing anything criminal. I guarantee it."

Brant didn't want to believe him. He pushed down the hope that flared to life and looked away. "What the hell do you know about women?"

He chuckled earthily. "You think I don't enjoy the company of women just because I live up here in the woods?"

Brant snorted because he knew perfectly well that Mack had his share of female company. Hell, he came to Denver often enough to find that company, not wanting to deal with the problems that came with having an affair with someone in his town.

"You don't know Gianna."

There was a pause, then Mack shook his head. "I only met her at Thanksgiving. So yeah, you probably know her better than I do. But in my line of work, I have to bet my life on quick judgements and my money bets she didn't steal anything. If she did, it was accidental."

"I *heard* her," Brant stated firmly, wanting so badly for Mack's words to be true. But...

"What did you hear?"

"She didn't have enough of something. She was talking to her father and saying that she needed more time. I only heard one side of the conversation but she was pretty clear about needing more of whatever she hadn't gotten yet."

"So, you've convicted her on half of an eavesdropped conversation with her father?"

"She's been hiding something from me! Every time I walk into her office, she shoves something into her desk or under a stack of files."

"Do you know what?"

Brant stood up impatiently, stomping to the edge of the porch. It was colder here, away from the fire, but at least he had room to breathe. "If I knew what she was hiding, then I wouldn't be up here with you."

"Where would you be?"

He wasn't sure, which was part of the problem.

"You love her."

Brant swung around, startled. "I don't!"

Mack laughed. "Course you do. Otherwise, you'd be back in Denver, arresting her cute butt for whatever it is that you think she's done."

"I..." he didn't continue. Not because he wanted to deny Mack's words, but because he didn't know if they were true or if he was just...whatever. He wasn't sure about anything anymore.

"I'll have more information when my tech people go through her computer files and figure out which corporate reports she's downloaded over the past few weeks. If all of the data she's downloaded can be traced back to a particular report she created for the company, then everything is fine. But if there's something that doesn't make sense, well, then..."

"She's innocent," Mack declared, leaning back and swinging the wool scarf around his neck to ward off the cold. "What do you want to bet?"

Brant ignored his brother in favor of staring out at the woods, not really seeing any of the beauty of the mountain. His mind was thinking about Gianna and how she looked when she first woke up in the morning. And what she might look like if...no. He wouldn't go there. He wouldn't arrest her. No way!

So what the hell was he going to do?

Chapter 12

Gianna glared at the computer monitor, feeling like she'd just lost something precious. Brant had been gone for three days. He hadn't called or texted at all.

Had she done something wrong? Was their time together over? Should she call him again or just leave him alone?

From the moment she'd accepted that the sexual attraction wasn't going away between them, she'd accepted that their time together couldn't be long term. Brant just wasn't that kind of a man. He liked variety. She knew that and had...okay, so she hadn't accepted that about him. She'd hoped. She'd started to dream. She'd gone to that stupid store and...well, dreamed about something more. Something like what Selena had with Reid.

Gianna lifted her tote bag onto her lap, needing more tissues since she'd just used the last one on her desk. "Darn it!" she mumbled, digging through the contents of her purse. But there was too much in there and she couldn't find the tissues.

Grabbing the magazines, she angrily whipped them out of her purse and...

"What's wrong?" a soft voice asked.

Gianna glanced up, her red-rimmed eyes peering through teary lashes at her friend. "Selena!" she gasped, shoving the magazines back into her tote bag and shoving everything under her desk. The magazines were bad enough, but the box...no way could she allow Selena to know about that box! Selena was a wonderful person and a good friend, but she was married to Reid. She couldn't ever let Selena know about the secret box in her purse!

It was silly and...she really shouldn't have done it. But all was not lost. She could just return it and everything would be fine. No one would ever know!

"What's in your bag?" Selena teased. "Obviously something you don't want me to know about."

Gianna sighed as her shoulders slumped. "Nothing important. Just..."

"Show me," Selena urged. "You know I can't stand not knowing about a secret." She plopped down in the only chair in Gianna's office, smiling to her friend.

Gianna looked down at her desk, unable to look at her beautiful, happy friend. She couldn't admit how silly she'd become lately. Silly and hopeful and just...stupid! "You don't want to know."

"Of course I do. You're my friend and you look as if someone has died." Selena stopped abruptly. "Everyone is okay, aren't they? Is your family...?"

Shocked, Gianna shook her head. "No, no one died. Everyone fine and is healthy." She paused and thought about her mother's heart issues. "At least, as far as I know...my parents haven't told me anything new. But..." she shook her head and looked down. "I just..."

"Why have you been crying?" Selena asked softly. "Tell me, Gianna. You know it won't go any further. I won't tell anyone."

Gianna blinked back a fresh wave of tears, not sure what to do.

"Just think of me as your big sister," Selena joked. "In fact, why don't you come over tonight for dinner and you can show me how to make fresh pasta?"

Gianna laughed. "You don't want to learn to make fresh pasta."

"Of course I do! The stuff you made for me last week was incredible! I've never had pasta that tasted better than that."

"I'm glad that you liked it," Gianna replied, "but…"

"No buts – you are coming over." Selena reached under Gianna's desk and grabbed her friend's purse. "Come on, we'll…"

Selena stopped, staring at the contents that had fallen out of Gianna's bag. "Is this…?" she whispered, pulling the magazine out and looking at the titles. "Oh, Gianna! Has Brant…?"

"No," she replied and took the bridal magazines back, then reached into her purse and pulled the other three bridal magazines out. She stared at them for a long moment, her heart aching. With a frustrated sob, she dumped them all in the garbage can. "What I thought was something more, something wonderful," she admitted with a sniff, "is over. He is gone."

"Reid said he was just visiting his brother in the mountains," Selena argued.

Gianna stared at her friend for a long moment. Brant had told her that he was on a business trip. But he'd actually gone to stay with his brother? In the mountains? What did that mean?

She knew exactly what it meant. The last small kernel of hope died with that news. Lowering her head so that Selena didn't see the new tears, she pulled her tote over her shoulder. "I have to go. I'm sorry about the pasta, but I will teach you *un'altra notte, si?*" And she left, not waiting for an answer. She just needed to leave the office and find a place to hide.

Tomorrow. Tomorrow she could deal with life and figure out how to move on. But for now, she needed to hide.

Selena watched her friend hurry down the hallway. Gianna pressed the elevator call button, but when it didn't arrive immediately, she turned and hurried into the stairwell.

That was going to be a long walk down, Selena thought sympathetically, heading towards Reid's office. They were on the tenth floor of the building. Ten flights of stairs in Gianna's heels was going to be brutal.

"Hey," she called out, stepping into Reid's office. "When is Brant coming back?"

"Why?" Reid asked, standing up from his desk so that he could wrap his arms around her.

"Because Gianna was upset about something. She won't tell me what but…"

"Stay out of this," Reid warned, adding a kiss to soften the message.

Selena pulled back, but she didn't step out of his arms. "Stay out of what? What's going on? Why is Brant visiting Mack when Gianna is so upset? Did he do something?" Her eyes narrowed as she looked up at her husband. "Did he break up with her? Is that why she's crying?"

"He didn't break up with her. At least, not officially."

She rested her hands on his shoulders, confused. "Maybe you should fill in the missing pieces."

Reid shook his head. "I can't. Not yet anyway."

Selena wanted to question him further, but someone knocked on Reid's office door. They both turned to find a tech guy standing in the doorway, holding a folder.

"I'm sorry to disturb you, sir. But I can't find Brant and he asked me to bring this to him as soon as I had it."

Reid nodded and extended his hand. "I'll make sure that he gets it."

The man gave the folder to Reid and quickly retreated. Selena peered around her husband's arm curiously. "What's that about?"

He didn't try to hide the report as he skimmed down the page. "It's a list of the data that someone has downloaded over the past few weeks. But this doesn't give me the information Brant wanted."

"What was he looking for? I'm sure Gianna could get it for him."

Reid sighed and turned, pulling her back into his arms. "Honey, the information is about Gianna. Brant thinks that she's been spying on the company, stealing information."

Selena stared wide-eyed up at her husband for a long moment before bursting into laughter, shaking her head as she pulled away. "No," she laughed. "Um..." lifting a finger, she gestured for him to wait. It took her a few more moments to get her amusement under control, but finally, she turned to look up at him. "Okay, so let me get this straight: Brant thinks Gianna is stealing company information?"

"Right. Brant couldn't figure out what Gianna was hiding. This report was supposed to give us a clue."

"And Gianna thinks that they've broken up?"

Reid's eyes were emotionless and Selena knew that meant he was conflicted. He wasn't sure what to think.

"I can't confirm that. I haven't spoken to her in the past few days."

Selena took her husband's hand. "Come with me." She led him down the hallway to Gianna's office. The light was still on since Gianna hadn't taken the time to turn it off in her rush to get out of the office. "This is what she was hiding," Selena announced, gesturing to the trash can.

Reid looked around, not sure what was wrong. He didn't notice the magazines, trying to figure out what his wife was telling him. "Are you saying that Gianna used a different computer?"

Selena blinked, not sure where he was going with that. "Another computer? You have excellent security, Reid." She huffed slightly. "No, I'm not talking about what you and Brant think of her. I'm trying to show you what Gianna thought of her relationship with Brant."

Reid still looked confused.

She laughed and lifted up on her toes, kissing him briefly before pulling away. "You're handsome and brilliant in many ways. But in others, you're clueless." So instead of asking him to guess again, she pulled the bridal magazines out of the trash, handing them to him. "I suspect that this is what Gianna was trying to hide from Brant." She leaned forward. "There is no corporate espionage. Just a woman in love with a man, Reid. And I have to tell you that Gianna has plans. Big plans. Plans that didn't include staying here in Denver. So if she was thinking along these lines," she said, once more pointing to the magazines, "then she'd fallen hard for Brant. Harder than even I knew."

Reid stared hard at the magazines covered in flowers and beautiful, happy brides. "This is what she kept shoving out of sight?" he muttered. He flipped through the magazines briefly, then looked at his wife, his expression changing from confused to amused. "Oh, he's going to be kicking himself sideways when he finds out."

Selena shook her head and grabbed the magazines. "Oh no! You're not telling him about these," she said and dumped them back into the trash. "Come on, dear."

Reid frowned over his shoulder at the trashcan, thinking that he should tell Brant about them.

"No!" Selena warned. "We're going home. Besides, I tried to convince Gianna to show me how to make pasta, but she was too upset. So now, you're going to cook me dinner."

Reid pressed the button for the elevator, smiling down at her but his expression was more wolfish than pleasant.

"Ah, so dinner is *my* choice, right?"

Instantly, Selena knew where his mind was going. And just as fast, her body responded to that idea liking it. A lot! But still, a woman had to play hard to get, even if it was with her husband, right? "No, you can't have me for dinner!" Her rejection was tempered when she moved closer to Reid, stepping into his arms and smiling up at him.

Chapter 13

Brant watched with increasing dread as Reid's Jeep pulled up next to his sedan. He'd been here for four days and knew that Mack was getting ready to toss him out.

Yeah, it was time to go back. No matter what she'd done, it was time to face the real world. But he'd come to one conclusion. He loved her. He didn't care what Reid or the tech people found, he wasn't letting her go to jail.

Now, it was time to face his brother and find out what Reid had discovered.

"You look like crap," Reid announced cheerfully as he walked up the stairs to Mack's cabin. "Lose your razor?"

Brant reached up and smoothed the rough beard that he'd ignored for the past few days. "I think it suits me," he replied.

Reid shook his head. "Right. You keep on telling yourself that." He sighed and handed Brant the papers. "Here's what we found."

Brant stared at the file, not wanting to touch it. But Reid patiently waited until he accepted the folder. And still, he walked over to the porch chairs and slumped down into the closest one, not bothering to open the file.

"What's in it?" he asked, not wanting to hear, but knowing he needed to know in order to protect Gianna.

"The tech guys are good. They were able to list all of the data she'd downloaded over the past few weeks, including the search history on her computer. Not hard to do, but still, they thought of everything." He nodded towards the file. "Go ahead. Open it and take a look."

Brant stared at the seemingly innocuous folder for another long moment, then sighed and accepted that it was time. He'd avoided reality for long enough.

He read through the first page, which was just a list of the Internet sites she'd visited over the past few weeks. At first, it was simple things, such as translation sites, American idiomatic phrases, different cultures in various parts of the country. Then there was a slew of football sites. Brant knew that the searches were from when she'd been trying to learn about American football and he chuckled at some of the site names.

"She was bored, wasn't she? I told you that she needed more work." Reid grabbed Brant's beer and took a long swallow.

Brant nodded, agreeing with his brother. He even acknowledged that the work Gianna had done had always been exceptional. She was precise, careful, detail oriented, and figured out both the micro details and the big-picture issues.

As he skimmed through more of the searches, he was startled to see the odd wedding dress search pop up. And then more bridal advice sites, wedding lists, timelines...

"What the hell is all of this?" he demanded, furious that she would be thinking of weddings if...

He looked up, staring at his brother. Reid only lifted his eyebrows, waiting for penny to drop. Mack stepped out, carrying three beers, which he handed around before sitting down to watch.

"Is that the proof that Gianna hadn't done anything wrong?"

Brant didn't look up as he turned the page, but he took a moment to say, "Shut up," to his brother before focusing back on the lists. There were more wedding sites, but one of them included "How to Propose!" But the worst was the last few search requests.

"How to get over a hard breakup" and "When your man betrays you." There were more, each more painful to read than the last.

He flipped through the search results and focused on the data downloads. Every single one he could match up to reports he'd asked her to build for him. There wasn't anything out of the ordinary.

"This doesn't show any of the stuff that she stole. Where's the rest?"

Reid lifted his hands in the air. "That's it. That's all they found." He took a long sip of his beer. "Although, I was shown a bunch of bridal magazines that had been dumped into the trashcan. Any idea what that might be about?"

Brant was confused. "Bridal magazines? She was looking through bridal magazines?"

Reid nodded. Mack smirked. "Told ya."

Brant was more than ready to slug his younger brother, but he was too focused on trying to figure out what he'd missed.

"You were trying to figure out what she was hiding, idiot," Reid filled in for Brant. "She didn't want you to know that she was looking at bridal magazines."

Brant snapped the file folder closed, shaking his head. "But she was so secretive."

"Of course she was. Gianna probably thought you'd run to the hills if you found out that she was dreaming about marriage," Mack told him. Reid chuckled and the brothers tapped their beer bottles together.

"Good one, bro," Reid said.

Brant looked at both of them. "You're both idiots."

Reid lifted his eyebrows. "*We're* idiots?" He turned to Mack. "Am I the one moping on a mountain top because he's in love with a woman he erroneously thinks is a criminal?"

116

"I don't believe that is you," Mack said in a mocking tone, then both brothers turned to face Brant.

He lifted his hands in the air in defeat. "Fine!" He leaned back, taking a long swallow of his beer as he glared into the crackling fire pit. "So..."

"She's in love with you!" Reid announced loudly before Brant could come up with another theory. "She loves you and you're in love with her. She wants to get married! That's all she was hiding!"

"Which is why you came up here to escape from your feelings," Mack added. "But one thing I've known about my mountain. You can easily become lost in the woods, but you can't really lose your feelings. They stick with you no matter how far you hike."

Reid looked at his baby brother. "That's so profound of you," he teased.

"I'm a profound fellow," he came right back. They laughed at their quip, then turned to look at Brant. "So any sage words of advice for our man over there?"

Reid shook his head. "Shave, perhaps."

"Hell yeah! And do it before Gianna sees you," Mack agreed.

"Good point."

Mack nodded. "Good. Now that we've agreed on that, how do we get those love birds back together?"

Brant didn't argue with his assessment. "I need to go find Gianna."

"Not tonight, bro," Mack announced. "There's a snow storm coming our way. There's no way you'll make it down before it starts. And in your car, you'd slide into a tree and it would be ugly. So you're here for another night."

"But..."

"Come on," Mack interrupted. "We can walk down to The Bull Frog. It will at least get you out of my house for a few hours. You can socialize or brood about your stupidity, whichever floats your boat. But you're getting out of here so someone can tell you how ugly you look with that beard."

Brant rolled his eyes. "The weather forecast doesn't have any snow coming."

All three brothers looked up into the sky where stars twinkled in the inky night sky.

"Trust me. Snow is coming. Nothing huge, but enough to make the roads slick and dangerous. Especially in your pointless car."

"My car isn't pointless," Brant argued, but knew that his brother was a weird sort of human weather gauge. If he said that snow was on the way, it would be snowing very soon. So instead of getting into his car to head back to Denver, the three of them walked down the gravel road that led to the town of Minneville. "It drives great in the city."

"Pointless up here," Mack asserted firmly. "Can't go over gravel or rocks or..."

"Hey, just because you have to drive over boulders to catch the bad guys or save the damsel in distress, that doesn't mean that my car is pointless."

"Actually, it's pretty rare that I have to save a damsel," Mack told his brothers. "The ladies who come out to hike are more sensible than their male counterparts. They do their research and figure out a plan, check in with me or Ryan at the Ranger's station and they're smart about where they hike."

"Why's that?"

Mack shrugged. "I don't know but I like it. I don't worry about the ladies. It's the men who I constantly worry about and it's idiot men who go out hiking, thinking that they know what they're doing, don't check in with us, and just head out into the woods. So, finding them is always more difficult."

"Yes, but where would the world *be* without us men?"

Mack grinned. "In a world of hurt," he agreed.

The walk to town was easy and The Bull Frog was a bar or pub, whatever one wanted to call it, with a quirky atmosphere that catered to both the locals and the tourists. During the summer months, the place was packed with hikers and people trying to fish in the cold waters that ran down the slopes of The Rocky Mountains to form rushing creeks and rivers as the streams merged. During the winter months, the skiers and snow lovers swarmed in. There were only a few months out of the year when things slowed down a bit and December was one of them. So when they stepped through the doors, the bar was crowded, but not as packed as it would be in a month or two. Finding a table near the back was relatively easy and, as they sat down, the owner, a beautiful, tall blond woman named Cynthia, walked over and smiled welcomingly at them. "Hey Mack! I haven't seen you around in a few days. Where have you been?"

"Trying to soothe my brother's tortured soul," he replied.

"Doesn't the mountain do that already?" she teased, as she set a pitcher of beer and three glasses down.

"Apparently, his soul was more tortured than even the mountain could fix."

She laughed, her long, blond hair shimmering in the overhead lights. "I didn't think that was possible," she replied, then turned to wink at Brant before walking away.

"She's nice," Reid observed as he poured beer. "And fast. I like a woman who brings me beer."

Mack punched Reid's arm. "Don't be a sexist ass."

Reid laughed. "Yeah, don't tell Selena I said that. She'd take me down in a heartbeat."

"We'll hold it over your head for when we need to blackmail you."

"Fair enough," Reid agreed.

Mack and Reid leaned back in their chairs, watching the crowd, grunting at the soccer game playing on one of the televisions that were set up in a corner. The sound was turned off so that the music of the bar could be heard, but the guys didn't need to hear the announcers to know what was happening on the field.

Reid and Brant drank most of the beer, which was a local craft brew and tasted a hell of a lot better than what was generally served in small towns. But Mack barely sipped his beer. Reid and Brant knew that their youngest brother rarely drank, especially when he was in town. He might be officially off duty, but as sheriff of a small town, he was never *really* off-duty. He had deputies, but Mack was always vigilant. And too often, the tourists on vacation drank too much and caused problems.

Sure enough, the brothers watched as a group of men, obviously hikers from their boots and attire, stepped through the doors.

Not by word or sound did Mack indicate that he was expecting trouble. But Brant and Reid knew that he was watching the four men.

They took a table over by the window, laughing loudly about their day, bragging about one thing or another while putting the other guys down. Typical male bonding.

Immediately, Cynthia stepped up to their table and smiled. "What can I get you boys?" she asked, being her usual friendly self.

One of them ordered two pitchers of beer and Cynthia left to fill the order.

"She seems nice," Brant commented of the tall, leggy blond. "Why couldn't I have fallen for someone less complicated?"

Mack chuckled. "Buddy, if you think that Cynthia is uncomplicated, you're nuts."

"She's a mess?"

"Nah. She's great. Cynthia is kind and easy-going, loves the mountains as much as anyone else and is friendly. But she has her demons, just like the rest of us."

"You dated her?" Reid asked.

"Never. We're just good friends." Mack looked over at the woman in question, long, blond hair cascading over her shoulder and a ready smile for everyone. She wore an old tee-shirt that had been washed so many times, it was soft and faded. Her jeans were the same, faithfully cupping her pert butt and long legs. Cynthia was the kind of woman that one might find on the beaches of California. Tall and slender, curvy in all the right places and silky blond hair paired with an easy, relaxed smile.

Until....

Cynthia delivered the pitchers of beers to the guys, but one of them smirked up at her with a dangerous look in his eyes.

Brant watched, tensing as he waited. He had no intention of allowing anyone to be fondled by a drunken bastard.

Sure enough, the stupid ass reached around, pretending to put his arm around Cynthia's waist. Brant was about to stand up and slam the guy against the wall for daring to touch the woman who was just trying to serve them, when the man's fingers were captured and viciously twisted by Cynthia. With a slow, incredibly sexy smile, Cynthia bent down low so she could whisper in the offender's ear.

Whatever she said caused the man in question to nod quickly as he sank lower in his seat. His face was a painful shade of red. Slowly, she released the man's fingers and stepped away. "If any of you need anything else, just let me know!" Cynthia smiled, winked cheekily at the man across the table whose mouth was hanging open, then walked away with her chin held high.

"Damn, that was impressive!" Brant whispered.

Reid whistled, nodding in agreement. A split second later, the bar erupted in applause and Cynthia spun around, glaring at the others who were making such a big deal out of the interaction. "Yeah yeah! Get it over with!" she announced.

The bar patrons laughed and the applause actually increased. The only one not applauding was the guy who was shaking his fingers, trying to get circulation back to them.

Cynthia blushed, but took it all with good humor, even bowing to everyone before turning back to head into the kitchen.

"She's nice," Brant commented, but immediately thought about Gianna's dark curls and voluptuous body. Unfortunately, Cynthia just didn't do anything for him.

So much for an uncomplicated life.

"He's thinking about Gianna again, isn't he?" Reid asked.

Mack grunted, punching Brant's arm lightly. "You'll see her tomorrow. Snap out of it."

Brant glared at his brothers. "I think you are full of it about the snow. There's no reason..."

Mack lifted his eyebrows and Brant paused, then shut up as the three of them turned to look through the big window.

"Damn snow!" someone grumbled as a new customer stepped into the bar, brushing the first flakes of snow off his shoulders.

Brant and Reid turned to look outside. They could just make out the snow filtering out of the sky from the lone street light.

When they turned to face Mack again, they both had stunned expressions on their faces. "How do you *do* that?!" they both asked almost simultaneously.

"It's a gift," he teased, adding an "aw shucks" shrug.

A moment later, Mack groaned as the door opened. Reid and Brant immediately shifted to see what the new threat was. But the familiar face didn't give them any new information. The tall, sandy blond haired man standing in the doorway wasn't a threat.

"Isn't that Ryan, your friend?" Brant asked.

Reid was confused as well. "And a ranger? I thought you law enforcement types stuck together and were all buddies?"

"I am friends with Ryan," Mack answered, watching the man who looked around the bar, his eyes landing on the man who had tried to cop a feel on the pretty waitress.

"Ryan!" Mack called out.

It took a long moment for the ranger's intense glare to pull away from the idiot. A moment later, Ryan nodded in acknowledgement of his friend, but still hesitated to come over.

Mack stood up and walked over to the bar, grabbed another glass before walking back to their corner table. He poured some beer into it before lifting it invitingly towards Ryan, an obvious invitation to his friend.

Brant watched as the tall man walked over to their table. Ryan Dalton wasn't a man to mess with. He was as big and powerful as any of his brothers, but with a look about him that said, "Don't piss me off." Few ever dared. Any that did paid the price. A former Navy SEAL, Ryan was just as protective of the mountains as Mack was about his town and everyone who came for a visit. Was there a territorial gene embedded in the DNA of all law enforcement officers? Or was it learned?

Mack and Ryan muttered some greeting and the four of them started talking, but Brant wondered if there was something going on between Ryan and the pretty waitress. When he and his brothers had walked into the bar, she'd come right over with a smile and a pitcher of beer. Her friendly, open attitude seemed natural and the rest of the customers received the same friendly, efficient service.

But as soon as Ryan had walked in, Cynthia had taken one look at him and stalked into the kitchen. She hadn't appeared back in the main area of the bar again.

Their beer ran out and Reid looked around for Cynthia.

"She won't come back out," Ryan explained.

Mack laughed, slapping his friend on the back. "Did you piss her off again?"

Ryan grinned. "Eh, she loves me," he shrugged dismissively.

"Yeah, that's why we're not getting any more beer," Reid laughed.

Ryan chuckled, but he took out a ten dollar bill and grabbed the empty pitcher. "I know how to get her back out here," he said and walked over to the bar, serving himself. He slapped the money onto the cash register and carried the pitcher of beer back to their table.

Sure enough, Cynthia immediately stepped out of the kitchen, glaring daggers at the man. But she took the money and made change. But did she bring the change back to their table? Not a chance! Instead, she slapped the money onto the cash register, exactly where Ryan had left the ten dollar bill. The message was clear. Cynthia didn't want the man's change for a tip, and there was no way in hell she was going to bring the man his change either.

Ryan got the message and smiled tauntingly over the rim of his glass, clearly issuing a challenge to the pretty blond.

"Would you two get a room already?" Mack grumbled.

Reid and Brant chuckled as well, while Ryan just sat back, stretching his long legs out and pretending to relax. But Brant knew that the man wasn't relaxed. Just like Mack, he was fully alert and barely sipping his beer, ready to spring into action for any reason.

Brant shook his head slightly. He'd played poker with Ryan before and knew the man to be smart and quick. Both Mack and Ryan had several awards and both had been offered positions with other law enforcement agencies. But they loved this mountain and the people who came to enjoy it. They felt a deep sense of duty and protectiveness. They'd never leave. Besides, Brant preferred knowing that Ryan had Mack's back when trouble came up. They worked together whenever something went wrong, the two in sync with each other. And they knew these mountains better than anyone in the area. When trouble arrived, Mack and Ryan would fix it.

They stayed another hour, but by then, the bar was starting to slow down, the tourists heading back to their cabins so they could get an early start the next morning.

On the walk back to Mack's place, Brant thought about seeing Gianna tomorrow. He'd been wrong. So damn wrong, but she didn't know what he'd thought. He could fix this, he told himself. He'd abandoned her and hadn't responded to her texts. But somehow, he'd convince her to give him another chance. The idea of her staying in Denver and not being able to see her, to talk to her and laugh with her, hold her in his arms every night for the rest of his life, was too desolate to think about. He just...he couldn't think that.

And there was no way he would let her fly back to Italy. She might be homesick, but he'd help her build a home here. He knew that she loved the United States, had tried to learn about the American culture. Perhaps he could tempt her with other lessons, or just...hell, he had no idea.

All he knew was he couldn't lose her!

Chapter 14

Gianna stared blankly at the screen without seeing the numbers. At the moment, her heart was in shreds and all she wanted to do was run back to Italy and be surrounded by the warmth of her family. Her mother would make fresh bread while her father made pasta with sauce and whatever else he'd found at the market that morning. Her brothers and sisters would rush over and tease her until she smiled and started laughing.

But Gianna couldn't imagine ever laughing again. She wanted to curl up into a ball and ignore the world.

What had she done wrong? Everything had seemed so blissfully wonderful only four short days ago. Had she said or done something? Had he seen the bridal magazines?

That was probably it, she thought.

Well, if that's the case, then she didn't need him! If he was afraid of a relationship, especially a permanent one, then he needed to tell her that he wasn't looking for long term. He should be honest with her and not just...disappear!

A tingling sensation suddenly crept up her arms. Turning, she found Brant standing in her office doorway looking...rough. He'd lost weight and seemed to have forgotten to shave in the past few days.

"I'm sorry," he whispered as he stepped into the room.

An apology? She stood up and grabbed some file folders. "Sorry for what?"

Holding the folders like a shield, she forced herself to look up at him. Her heart pounded in her chest and she could feel words trying to crawl up her throat, she wanted to say she didn't need forever or marriage or any of it.

But that would be dishonest.

"I'm sorry for leaving."

Gianna shrugged. "No problem. It's nothing," she flicked her fingers in a very Italian way as if dismissing the issue completely. "I have a meeting," she told him.

He stepped closer to her, still blocking the doorway. "Can we talk about it tonight? Over dinner?" He smiled. "I promise not to make any messy American foods."

Gianna pressed her lips together, not allowing herself to laugh or even feel the warmth of his body so close. She wanted to throw herself into his arms and feel his strength surround her, but she backed up, not giving in to that temptation.

"I'm sorry. I have plans tonight."

She didn't, but there was no way she was going to admit it.

"What are you doing? I could..."

"No," she asserted. "I have plans tonight and they won't end until late." She shifted the files in her arms. "And right now, I am going to be late for my meeting." She frowned up at him, daring him to continue to stand in her way.

Thankfully, he stepped back, giving her room to leave.

She hurried down the hallway to the conference room. Everyone was already seated, but thankfully, the meeting hadn't started. She took a seat at the end of the table and pulled out her notes. But as the group started talking, she struggled to concentrate.

She should have asked. Gianna's pen was poised over a fresh sheet of paper, prepared to take notes, but nothing was registering to her brain. In the back of her mind, she heard the other meeting participants conversing, but she couldn't add anything to the topic.

Shaking her head, she tried to push Brant's apology out of

her mind. She didn't want to think about him. Gianna had been worrying about him constantly for the past several days, and wracking her brain, trying to figure out what she'd done to push him away.

Now he comes back to town, apologizes and expects everything to be just wonderful? No way! She wasn't that kind of a woman!

"Are you okay, Gianna?" someone asked.

Gianna looked up at the others at the conference room table, startled to see every eye pointed at her. "*Mi dispiace*," she whispered. "I'm sorry."

A few people smiled, seeming to understand that she was upset about something. Thankfully, the others turned and continued the meeting. When it was over, Gianna grabbed up her papers and hurried out the door, her head bowed as she made her way back to her desk.

Closing her office door, she sank down into her chair and tried to pull herself together. "This isn't going to work! You have got to snap out of this!" she whispered fiercely to herself.

But by the end of the day, her supervisor had returned three reports with errors, asking her to re-do them and turn them in tomorrow. Plus, she'd been so distracted that she hadn't even gotten through her e-mail messages, she still had several issues to fix in the data she'd inputted yesterday and the marketing department needed the latest sales data for the north-east retail sites, a report she should have sent to them three days ago.

Instead of handling the issues, which she'd probably mess up anyway, she gathered up her belongings, stuffed everything into her tote bag and...her fingers touched the box that was still at the bottom of her purse. Over the past few days, she'd told herself to return it but...she hadn't.

"*Accidenti!*" she muttered and angrily swiped at the tears sliding down her cheeks. Why hadn't she returned the contents of that stupid box! Stupid! She paused and took several deep breaths. When she felt as if she could walk out of the building without stumbling, she nodded her head and tossed her bag over her shoulder.

Once again, she bowed her head as she headed to the elevators. But once there, she discovered too many others waiting for the elevator so she forced a smile for her co-workers and headed directly for the stairs.

Brant watched Gianna walk down the hallway, cursing himself for what he'd done to her. His stupidity had turned a vibrant, beautiful woman into a shadow of herself. She used to walk down the hallway with a bounce to her step, smiling and greeting everyone she ran into. There wasn't a person on this floor who she hadn't befriended. And now she couldn't even ride the elevators with them. She hid herself away, bowing her head as if she needed to become smaller than she was.

"She's hurting," Reid sighed, stopping right next to him. "You haven't fixed this yet."

Brant turned away from his brother, blurting out a few choice expletives. "Go away," he growled when Reid followed him into his office.

"When are you going to fix this?" Reid demanded, crossing his arms over his chest as he glared at his brother.

"I tried!" Brant yelled. "First thing this morning, I went to her office and apologized."

"And?" he asked.

He rubbed a hand over his face. "She accepted my apology, then told me that she needed to get to a meeting."

"Do it again."

Brant leaned back in his leather chair, glaring right back at his brother. "I asked her if I could take her out to dinner tonight and explain. She said no, she had plans."

Reid's eyes widened. "You're letting her go out with another man?"

Absolute silence followed that question. Brant stared at his brother, his muscles tightening as he considered that possibility. "No." The word was spoken softly, but with absolute authority. "No way!"

And with that, he exploded out of his chair, grabbed his car keys, and stalked out of his office with a determination he hadn't felt in a long time.

The possibility that Gianna was dating someone else hadn't occurred to him, but just the thought made his blood boil. Yeah, he'd messed up. But no way was he letting Gianna be with another man.

Unless...was she not in love with him? Had she moved on?

Brant thought about the way she'd touched him, the look of bliss in her eyes whenever he made love to her. No, he thought with certainty. Gianna had fallen for him just as hard as he'd fallen for her.

So, why the hell had he believed her capable of stealing?

He'd been a complete and utter idiot, he thought.

"Damn it!" and he sped through the evening traffic, heading to her building.

Once there, he took the stairs two at a time, furious with her for moving on to date another man! How could she? Why would she? Had her feelings been that shallow? That superficial?!

"Gianna? Open the damn door!" he bellowed, pounding on her door.

Gianna jumped at the sudden commotion. Fury, rich and powerful, surged through her at his insistence.

Ignoring her flour covered hands, she marched to the door and threw it open, relieved to be angry instead of the soul-deep depression she'd fallen into.

As soon as she saw him, her fury erupted. *"Non attaccare la mia porta in quel modo! Hai idea di cosa potrebbero pensare i vicini? Questo è un quartiere tranquillo e sei una persona orribile e horribile! Ti odio più di quanto abbia mai pensato di poter odiare qualcuno! Se non ti rivedrò mai, sarà troppo presto!"*

Brant smiled, relieved to see her here alone, looking so painfully beautiful that he ached to pull her into his arms. "I have no idea what you just said, but I don't care. I love you, Gianna! I love you and I'm sorry that I was such an idiot."

She stared up at him for a long moment, not moving. Not even her flour dusted curls moved. For once, her entire being was still with shock.

When he stepped into her apartment, she jerked out of her trance, backing up quickly. "I call you an idiot and that I don't want to ever see you again, and you tell me you love me?"

Brant laughed, relief surging through him. She was cooking, which he knew she did in order to relax. Or to feel better. Or to get herself out of a funk. Gianna cooked all the time, actually, so perhaps her cooking wasn't indicative of anything, but he attributed her cooking to her wanting him close by. And missing him.

"I had no idea what you just said, so yeah. I guess I told you that I loved you when you were cussing me out."

She lifted a flour-covered hand. *"Uno momento!"* She moved to the stove, stirring something in a big pot. But she wasn't really stirring. She was thinking. And because she wasn't kicking him out, he walked over to stand close to her. From a few inches away, he could smell the sweet scent of her perfume. Or maybe it was her shampoo, he wasn't sure. But she smelled good. Like vanilla and basil. Not something he would ever have thought to combine before, but on Gianna, it was perfect.

She realized how close he was and peered over her shoulder. "Say what you want to say and get out," she snapped at him.

"I want *you*," he told her.

He heard the sharp intake of her breath, but she didn't respond. For several seconds, she stirred the contents of the pot. Finally, she shook her head. "You had me. You left me. You rejected me, and now you can't have me. Never again."

He trailed a long finger down her spine and watched her shiver. Not just that, the spoon jerked, splattering red sauce all over the white kitchen cabinets.

She spun around, pointing the red-sauced spoon at him like a sword, her eyes burning with fury and pain. "Don't you dare!" she snapped. "You cannot kiss me! You *no canna* touch me! You left me and you..." the tears sprang to her eyes again. "You hurt me! I no give you another chance to hurt me more!"

He leaned a hand on either side of the countertop, imprisoning her in his arms, but he didn't touch her. He could see in her eyes that she didn't want him to touch her.

"I'm sorry that I hurt you, Gianna. I wish I could say that it won't ever happen again. But it will. I'm an ass. And I suspect that you're going to hurt me too. After all, we are going to have years, hopefully decades, to fight with each other. And then we'll kiss and make up, then talk about what we did to hurt each other until the hurting stops. In between all of those fights," he paused, seeing the tears flow down her eyes, "I hope to make you laugh. I want to fill all of your days with happiness and wonder. I want to have kids with you and teach them how to play American football and soccer." He smiled at the irritated compression of her lips, but focused on what he needed to say.

"I messed up. I didn't trust you. It won't happen again, but

I'll make other mistakes. One thing I can promise you though, I won't ever leave you like I did these past few days again. And I'll also admit that I left because my feelings for you were too strong. I thought you'd done something illegal and I didn't want to be tempted to help you. I wanted to be strong and, in my mind, being strong meant being mean. Since then, I've come to understand that being strong means talking things through and being honest with you." He leaned closer. "I won't do it again. I can promise you that right here and now."

He stopped. Waiting. He wanted to hear what she might say to that, assuming that she'd want to know what he'd thought she'd done. So he wasn't expecting her to throw herself into his arms. Laughing, he pulled her in closer, burying his face in her soft curls. "Gianna, I'm so sorry!"

"You're right. You *are* an idiot!"

He chuckled, and flinched. "Gianna...do I have a wet spoon against my back?" he asked softly.

Her eyes widened as she realized that she was still holding the sauce-covered spoon which was, indeed, plastered against the white material of his dress shirt.

"I'm so..."

He stopped her with a kiss. And he didn't give a damn about his shirt or the pasta or the flour. She tossed the spoon onto the counter. But before she could kiss him back, the spoon toppled her tote bag off the countertop, spilling everything onto the floor.

"Your kitchen just gets more and more messy because of me," he teased.

Pulling out of his arms, Gianna surveyed her kitchen. It really was a mess now. But then she realized what was on the floor. The box!

Rushing over, she grabbed the box and hid it behind her back.

"Don't worry about this mess. Why don't you open a bottle of wine and..."

"Gianna, what's in the box?" he asked softly.

"You said you were going to trust me!" she gasped when he pinned her against the pantry door.

He chuckled. "I am going to trust you. And you're going to trust me. So whatever is in that box, I want to know about it."

She shook her head, flour filling the air as it fluttered from her hair. Gianna coughed slightly, but she didn't pull her hands from behind her back. "You don't need to know about it," she asserted firmly.

"Gianna, do you trust me?"

"Yes," she replied, indignant.

"I trust you too." He twirled a curl around on his finger. "A week ago, I would have thought that you were hiding something you stole from the company. From me. But now I'm sure that, whatever is behind your back is something else. And no, you don't need to show me, but I want to share my life with you." He kissed her gently. "Gianna, will you share your life with me? Not just your body or your smiles, but *everything*. I want to know your secrets and share mine with you. I want to have a family with you and meet your Italian family, so that they will know that you will be mine for the rest of our lives."

She burst into tears with his words.

"*Ti amo, Gianna. Ti amo tanto!*"

His declaration of love stopped the tears and she looked up at him with surprised delight. Slowly, she revealed the box. Lifting the lid, she revealed the diamond ring, set for a man, nestled amid the velvet. "I wanted to propose to you," she explained. "Just as an American woman might. But I started reading the magazines and women don't do that here. At least, not as much as I thought they did. So I messed up again."

He looked down at the diamond ring, more touched than he'd thought possible. "I love it! And yes, I will marry you, Gianna," he promised. He then reached into his pocket and pulled out a diamond ring, this diamond bigger but in a daintier setting. "Will you marry me?"

Gianna laughed through her tears, blinking so that she could focus on the ring. "Yes!" she gasped.

He took her hand, sliding the ring onto her finger. She did the same with his ring and she kissed his hand.

"I love you! I love you so much."

And with that, he lifted her into his arms, carrying her out of the messy kitchen and into her bedroom. The following morning, he called the office and told his assistant that they would both be out of the office for the next few days.

And he didn't answer his phone when his brother called. Brant was sure that Reid was only trying to yell at him for dumping all of the meetings on his schedule. Reid could deal with the pressure for a while.

Epilogue

"Come on! They are going to arrive any moment! We need to be there!" Gianna called, herding their two oldest boys out of the bathroom, having given up on trying to get their hair smoothed down. At six and four, Giovani and Antonio were too filled with energy to care about their thick, curly hair actually being in place.

"We're coming," Brant grumbled, hauling three year old Rebecca under his arm like a bag of potatoes. Obviously, he'd just caught her trying to escape because she had her usual mischievous grin as she bounced along under her father's arm.

"What did you do?" Gianna demanded, frowning at the bow she'd just put in her daughter's hair fifteen minutes ago.

"Daddy said it okay," she replied, adorable chubby cheeks adding to her impish look.

Brant lifted her up by the ankles so she was upside down. "Daddy did NOT tell you it was okay!" he admonished. "In fact, I believe I said no several times!"

Rebecca only giggled harder, loving the gentle handling by her father. The little girl had complete confidence that he wouldn't drop her. And there was the fact that she was the daredevil of the group.

"Fix her bow! She has to look pretty!" Gianna yelled. "And stop holding her like that. You're messing up her dress."

Brant pulled her up higher and Rebecca giggled harder. "Are you going to mess up again?" he asked her.

"Yes!" she yelped in between gasps of breath because she was giggling too hard.

"Then you're going to have to stay like this," he told her.

Gianna frowned at her husband, shaking her head. "You're not helping, Brant," she said, her accent thickening as she worried about her parents and siblings arriving from the airport.

"I know. I'm sorry."

She groaned. "You're not sorry and..." she turned, spotting her boys whispering in each other's ears "No!" she ordered both of them.

Giovani looked up, an innocent look plastered on his adorable features. "We haven't done anything."

"You're going to!" she declared. "And I'm telling you now, *no!* If you do whatever it is that either of you are planning to do, you will be in *so* much trouble!"

The doorbell rang and Gianna breathed a sigh of relief. "They are here!" she announced happily. She headed towards the front door, but turned and looked back at her family. The boys still looked innocent, which was always a bad sign. Her husband had at least turned Rebecca right side up, but she was still grinning like a loon. Another bad sign.

But then they all turned and looked at her, smiling and she stopped. Just absorbing the moment. For this one moment, her life was calm and quiet and peaceful.

The doorbell rang again and she laughed. Her life had very short moments of peace and tranquility surrounded by absolute chaos. Delightful, wonderful chaos.

"Fine! Get the door yourselves," she told her boys. They sprang into motion, rushing to the door to let in her parents and siblings along with their spouses and families. There would be twenty of them this Thanksgiving weekend. For some reason, they always wanted to come for Thanksgiving. Having twenty people in one house for four days was absolutely wonderful chaos. And they always served mashed potatoes. And pasta!

Excerpt to "Taming Mack"
Book 3, Sinful Nights Series
Release Date: February 15, 2019

"Who the hell are you?!"

Eve jumped, shocked by the angry demand. So far, she'd only received warm, friendly greetings from Cynthia's regular customers.

Turning to face the owner of the deep voice, her own anger sparked. He was tall, broad shouldered, intimidating and carried handcuffs, as well as a gun on his hip. The law enforcement badge softened the fear of that gun, but he was still scowling darkly, which caused her heart to flutter in a girly manner that irritated her more than the anger in his voice. The man might look exceedingly hot in that uniform, but that didn't give him the right to sound so angry towards her.

It took her several seconds to remember that this wasn't her place and alienating the sheriff might not be the best idea. Small towns meant gossip. At the moment, The Bull Frog, Cynthia's adorable little pub, was filled with locals, most of whom were curious about who would be covering while Cynthia was out of town.

Pasting a bright, hopefully friendly, smile on her face, she tucked the empty pitcher under one arm and extended her other hand. "I'm Eve, Cynthia's friend. I'll be helping out here until Mona is better."

He silently studied Eve for a long moment. So long that Eve felt more than a little awkward with her hand sticking out like that. Finally, the man moved closer, taking her hand and shaking it briefly. Very briefly.

"Sheriff Jones," he replied quietly.

Eve continued to smile, trying to ease the man's glare. He was so tall, well over six feet tall, and the heavy, brown jacket he was wearing made his shoulders look even more impossibly broad. The hat and the gun... delicious! And she couldn't forget those handcuffs! Not that she was into that sort of stuff. But if she were...into the handcuffs...she would really like to be handcuffed by this guy. Hmmm...maybe she *was* into the handcuffs after all. Blinking, she met his gaze and tried to focus her thoughts.

Okay, not productive, she scolded herself firmly. She wasn't attracted to him. Not even slightly. Another point, she hadn't done anything wrong. So, why was he snapping at her? Surely he couldn't read her mind and know that she found his handcuffs appealing! Because she didn't! Not...well, okay, maybe a little!

"When's Cynthia coming back?" he demanded impatiently, snapping her back to the conversation.

Eve stiffened at his belligerent tone. "I don't know." Eve moved closer, struggling to keep her hopefully-still-friendly smile in place. The whole pub was staring and she didn't enjoy being the center of attention. "She'll be gone for as long as she needs to be gone."

"You don't have to get back to work?"

Eve considered pointing out it was none of his business, but that small town issue raised its ugly head once again. "I'm a photographer. I can work anywhere. The wilds of Colorado will be an interesting change of pace for me."

Incredibly, the scowl on his too-handsome face deepened. Did the man even *know* how to smile? Was it a skill that had to be learned?

"You're a bit of a grumpy-Gus, aren't you?" she whispered,

leaning forward slightly. "How about if I get you a drink? A beer? Maybe some cheese fries?"

The man continued to glower at her and she shifted her feet, beginning to feel more than slightly self-conscious. "I'm on duty."

That made sense, with the uniform and all. "Well, why don't you come on back when you're off duty?" she offered. "I'm sure a big ole basket of something greasy will help loosen up that smile! I know it's in there somewhere."

She heard someone behind her chuckle and cringed. "Anyway, I'm not here to cause trouble, Sheriff," she said, thinking of the old western movies her father had loved. "I'm just covering for Cynthia." She pretended to salute. "No trouble at all, sir!" She even added a curtsy for good measure.

The man sighed, rolling his eyes. "I doubt you can help it," he muttered under his breath. In a louder voice, he warned, "Watch out for the Miller twins. I found them by your back door a few minutes ago."

Several groans were heard and Eve wondered what harm a couple of boys could do, but she nodded. "Got it. Miller twins. Trouble. No beer till you're off duty."

She could practically see the gears turning in his head as he tried to figure out if she was mocking him. But not by a twitch of her lashes did she betray herself. In the end, he didn't call her out and turned on his heel before heading out the door. "Snow's on the way."

Again, a wave of groans was heard and she looked around in surprise. "Snow?" She blinked. "But its April! Surely there can't..."

The laughter stopped her words, indicating that yes, in April, there definitely could be snow. "Okay, fine! Snow in April. That means fires. I need to stock up on marshmallows."

With that, she moved back to the bar. "How about you? Ready to try the lilac martini?"

Joe, a gruff old hunter who came up to the mountains on the weekend to fish, chuckled as he shook his head. There were only about three hundred residents of Minneville, she'd discovered. But that number swelled to over six thousand during the summer weekends and about half that number during the winter weekends. There were cabins all over the surrounding woods and most of the people who rented them came into town to eat and buy supplies for camping, skiing, fishing, hiking, or whatever else they might dream up to do.

Scanning the room, she knew that Annie could handle the tables, so Eve stayed behind the bar, pouring beers for the guys sitting on the tall stools, none of whom wanted to get close to her lilac martini. Go figure!

During a lull in the beer-pouring, she decided to be proactive about the menu. Cynthia and her mother had made The Bull Frog profitable over the years by offering not just beer, but also greasy, delicious, snack foods. Nothing complicated, but perennial favorites such as cheese fries sprinkled with bacon and sour cream or spicy wings. Unfortunately, the profits had dwindled recently and Eve was just the person to spice things up! Eve loved to experiment and wanted to try something different while she was here. Maybe a bit of variety would bring people in, adding a bit of excitement to the options.

"So what should we have on the menu tomorrow?" she asked, opening her computer and pulling up her favorite recipe website. Clicking through options, she pinned several ideas to a new board, tossing out ideas to the four guys sitting at the bar. "How about stuffed potatoes with gruyere cheese?" she offered up.

All four men looked at her as if she'd lost her mind.

"Okay!" she clicked a few more pictures. "Sweet potato bites with goat cheese and..." she didn't even finish that statement, the looks on their faces nixed that idea too. "Potato puffs?" She almost laughed at the horror on their whiskered faces, then took the empty mug of one guy, filling it up, sliding it down the polished bar and grabbing his three dollars before going back to her computer. She looked at the options, then at the men. Maybe I'm doing this wrong, she thought. "How about Bear Patties?" she offered, looking at the picture of the sweet potato slice with a dollop of goat cheese and cranberries sprinkled over it. The picture looked easy to create.

All four men tilted their heads slightly as if they were considering the possibility. "Yeah. I'd try a Bear Patty."

Eve rolled her eyes, thinking that some men never really grew out of their teen years. Make a guy think he was eating bear dung and he was all over it. Go figure!

"Okay, I'll try Bear Patties tomorrow night for an interesting appetizer. And what about a blue devil shot for a specialty drink?"

More grunts, but the men looked at each other, interest lighting up their eyes. "Cynthia never gave us specialty drinks," one of them admitted. "Might like a taste of a blue devil."

The others grunted their agreement and Eve pinned the cocktail to a board for future reference as well. She'd have to pour it into shot glasses instead of the pretty martini glasses that she'd found in the back of Cynthia's storage area, but she didn't mind. It would be nice to increase the revenues in this place. Eve had reviewed the accounting books last night and realized that Cynthia had barely managed to make ends meet over the past few months. Something had to change.

"Okay, patties and devils. Spread the word and we'll see if the offerings help anyone's hunting or fishing the next day."

The men obviously liked that idea. At least, she thought they were smiling. Some of them had beards so thick and wiry, it was hard to determine their expressions.

Three hours later, Eve was more than ready to call it a night. Only a half hour until closing and the place had slowly cleared out.

Most of the men wanted to get an early start, something about bears and watering holes...she didn't want to know.

"What the hell is a blue devil shot and how in the world to you think it might improve a man's chances of catching a trout?"

Eve spun around, dropping the dishrag she'd been using to dry her hands. Sure enough, the sheriff was back, his wide-brimmed hat tipped back so she could see his eyes more clearly this time. Nice, she thought. Just as handsome as she remembered. And oh boy, he still had those handcuffs!

She shook the thought away. "I must be tired," she muttered.

"You didn't answer my question."

Eve moved back behind the bar, thinking it was probably safer there. She couldn't reach the jerk to punch him in the nose for being rude again. Eve doubted the local law enforcement hottie would appreciate being punched. That would most likely qualify as "assaulting an officer", even if he deserved it.

Mack watched the delicately built woman carefully, noting the fatigue that slowed her step. Gone was the bright, sunshiny smile and the glowing eyes. This woman was wiped out. He wanted to tell her that he could get rid of the last two customers for her so she could close up and go to bed, but...well, he didn't want her hanging around Minneville. He wanted her gone. She was too delicate, sweet...and tempting. She was like a breath of fresh air and he didn't like it.

Yeah, he knew that he was grumpy at the moment, but he didn't care. His town didn't need a woman like her. She'd been here for less than two days, and already she was changing things up.

When she left, he knew that she'd leave behind a disaster in her wake and he wanted to protect the people who lived here. Their lives were tough enough already. No need to get them used to something and then have it ripped away.

The woman tossed that rag into the bar sink and leaned against the counter, arms spread out wide as she watched him. Blue eyes, he noticed. And dark, curly hair, pale skin, soft lips. Too soft. Everything about her was too soft.

It would be one thing if this woman were here only for a weekend. Yeah, he could manage that. He might even like her, if she was just here for a short visit. A visitor wouldn't stir things up. A visitor could be enjoyed and then he'd simply wave as she moved on to a life that was a bit more interesting than life up here in this small, mountain town. Winters were brutally cold and the summers were filled with tourists. Eve Henderson wouldn't make it here. Too soft.

"You ready for that beer, Sheriff?" she asked, trying to hide her exhaustion, but he could still see it. It was there and he had the crazy instinct to pull her into his arms and kiss her until he earned a real smile from her.

Damn, she was enticing!

"Nope. Seen the Miller twins yet?"

She paused, her head tilting slightly, which drew his gaze to the gentle curve of her neck. He wondered if she smelled as good as she looked.

"Honestly Sheriff, I'm not sure if I could tell the difference between any of the men around here. They all wear thick, flannel shirts, every one of them seems to be in a competition to grow the thickest beard possible, and by the time they've ordered their fifth beer, I doubt any of them could tell the difference between themselves and their neighbor. So no, I don't think I've seen these mischievous Miller twins although, if they were here tonight, they didn't introduce themselves."

Mack chuckled. "Fair enough. And no, I doubt either of the twins would take the time to introduce themselves to you, but you'll know them when you see them."

"Are they lost?" she asked, suddenly worried. "I know the temperature drops pretty fast out here once the sun goes down."

The sudden urge to pull her into his arms and bury his nose in her soft, dark mass of hair hit him square between the eyes. In reaction, he pulled back, refusing to even contemplate get involved with a woman who was going to be around only long enough to realize that she didn't fit in around here.

The question in her eyes pulled his mind away from the tempting scent of her hair. "No. They're not lost. Those boys know these woods better than anyone. I'll check in with their mother. They're probably home by now."

He tipped his hat towards her and tried to walk away, but her mouth falling open stopped his retreat. "What's wrong?"

Her mouth opened and closed. Mack suspected she had absolutely no idea of how tempting she looked.

"Did you just tip your hat back, Sheriff?" she asked, that distractingly sunny smile forming on her pretty, full lips. Lips that were still pink even though all of the lipstick he'd noticed earlier was gone. She actually looked prettier now, with her makeup worn off and the soft, overhead lights creating shadows on her pale skin.

It irked him that he was focused on trying not to kiss her and she was focused on his hat. What the hell is wrong with his hat? "I guess so. Was that wrong?"

That sexy smile widened. Then her pretty white teeth bit down on her plump lower lip. "No. Not wrong." She did that head tilt thing again. "It's actually pretty hot, Sheriff." With a wink, she turned around and headed over to the last two customers. For a long moment, he stood there, stunned while he enjoyed the soft sway of her hips.

Mack realized where his mind had gone and he shook his head. Sexy butts were not on his agenda tonight.

He stomped out of the bar, relieved by the bite of the cold night air hitting his face. What was it about her? Yeah, it had been a long, hard winter, but even during the cold months, he could make it down the mountain to one of the other towns and find female companionship when he needed it. He wasn't sex starved, but the way his body had reacted to her round curves and sweet smile, one would think he hadn't seen a woman in a decade!

19743973R00090

Printed in Great Britain
by Amazon